Ozma

Dorothy and
the
Giant Peach
A Trumpian Adventure in Oz

by

Calamum Nomen

Founded on and making fun of the famous Oz stories
by *L. Frank Baum*

Pmurt Press
2020

ISBN: 978-1-7345747-8-4

Interior Illustrations by
John R. Neill (1877-1943)
W.W. Denslow (1856-1915)
Calamum Nomen (not dead yet)

The Letter courtesy of *Unknown*

This book belongs to

List of Chapters

1: Stairway To Oz

2: A Grandiose Entrance

3: "My Beautiful General"

4: Rumors

5: China Country

6: Climate Change

7: Bullshit!

8: Cockwomble

9: Que Veritas?

10: Polychrome's Advice

11: A Handful Of Glinda

12: Next!

13: MOGA

14: Politicians

15: The Rigmaroles

16: The Unquenchable Rust

17: Hamburders & Cofefe

18: Hats

19: The Procession Of The Trump

20: Dorothy & Toto

21: Near Miss

22: Memories Of The Nome King

23: Somnium

24: The Shovel

25: Dorothy & Billina

26: The Gates Of The Emerald City

27: Theresa May

28: The Queen Of The Field Mice

29: Toto

30: You're Fired!

31: The Letter

32: The Speech

33: Taking Uncle Henry's Advice

34: The Loser

35: Taking Aunt Em's Advice

36: The Journey Home

37: Return From Oz

GLINDA.

Chapter 1
Stairway To Oz

In the Great Hall of the Emerald City Royal Palace sat a gathering of dear friends, exchanging stories and reliving adventures both new and old.

"Tell it again, Dorothy!" exclaimed the Scarecrow.

"Yes Dorothy, please tell us again about that strange little man and all his tomfoolery!" the Cowardly Lion pleaded.

"He certainly was a humbug, wasn't he?" the Tin Woodman chuckled.

Nearby, sitting in Her throne was Princess Ozma; Ruler of Oz, cheerfully chatting with Glinda; Good Witch of the South, who was reading from the Great Book of Records. They couldn't help but overhear the happy gathering and Princess Ozma giggled softly. Both had heard this story so many times that even they had lost count.

At that moment, a mild-mannered elderly man with thinning black hair and matching waistcoat appeared, seemingly out of thin air.

The gathering of friends erupted in cheers at his appearance.

"Talking about me, were you?" he inquired.

"How did you know?" Princess Ozma replied.

Just then, the elderly man, who everyone knew as the former Wizard of Oz, wiggled his fingers at his head, causing smoke to puff out from his ears.

"My ears were burning," he said with a straight face.

Dorothy, the Scarecrow and everyone else roared with laughter, including Glinda.

Only Princess Ozma remained stone-faced, or so She tried. It took all Her royal powers to stifle the laughter that so yearned to escape.

"I thought you were retired?" Her Majesty inquired, still on the verge of a giggle.

The former Wizard of Oz bowed deeply and rose slowly.

"A man has to have a hobby, Your Majesty," he replied.

That was all the Royal Ruler could take as a giggle began in low… then it started to grow.

In no time, Princess Ozma was in full-on giggle mode and unable to stop for several minutes.

The rest of the gathering joined in and the Great Hall of the Emerald City Royal Palace echoed with laughter… as it often did.

"What's this?" Glinda remarked as she gazed down into the Great Book or Records.

The Great Book or Records, which spells out every event that happens in Oz as it is happening, now spelled out the arrival of someone new to the Land of Oz.

"Someone from the Great Outside has just arrived," Glinda said matter-of-factly. She looked over at Princess Ozma, who knew that look very well and called for her Magic Picture.

In no time at all, several Handmaidens arrived with a beautiful framed picture that showed the Royal Ruler any place within or even outside of Oz in the numerous lands, oceans and deserts that surround the fairy kingdom.

"Show me the newcomer to Oz in the…" Princess Ozma began before pausing, "Where is this creature now?"

Glinda glanced down at the whisper thin pages, then returned Ozma's gaze.

"Quadling Country… on the Mountain of the Hammer-Heads," the Good Witch of the South replied.

The Magic Picture, upon hearing the location, displayed a curious scene.

Nestled on a plateau between two rocky peaks stood a staircase leading down below the clouds and rising towards a lone figure, bearing a shovel.

Just then, the elderly man came forward and studied the images playing out before him.

"Those look like Magic Stairs," he observed, "but how did he get them… and how did he get here?"

The retired Wizard of Oz was puzzled, especially since only Princess Ozma, Glinda; Good Witch of the South and he were permitted to perform magic in the Land of Oz.

This was, of course, a Royal Proclamation by Princess Ozma long ago after countless attempts to take over Oz by those who used magic for Evil means.

Chapter 2
A Grandiose Entrance

The lone figure stood erect, shovel in hand and puffing his chest out while pouting; his lower lip protruding as he stared intently at the scene before him.

His hair, copper-blonde in color, looked almost alive as it flew about in the stiff breeze coming off of the mountain peaks surrounding the Magic Stairs.

His skin had an almost orange tone to it, as though he had spent way too much time in the peach orchards of Quadling Country.

Dressed in ill-fitting formal clothing, he looked about as though trying to pick someone out of a crowd.

To his own eyes, there were adoring crowds surrounding him and swooning profusely at his every gaze. The wind sounded to him as cheers and a roar of approval, so the lone figure waved to his adoring crowds.

In the view of the Magic Picture, the lone figure was surrounded only by misty shadows, silence and a few of the Hammer-Heads who had been ordered to escort the stranger off of their mountain.

The Hammer-Heads were a curious race of creatures who lived on a high mountaintop in the southern Quadling Country of Oz. They were small in stature, with flattened heads, telescoping necks and no arms. Stubborn and reclusive by nature, they would refuse to negotiate, compromise or agree upon anything that caught their attention.

They were clearly agitated at the appearance of the lone figure with the curious hair... and yet, they appeared to render a small measure of respect by not pounding him mercilessly with their heads. In truth, it was probably the shovel he gripped tightly that they feared being struck by.

Just then, the lone figure stepped onto the moving stairway and began a slow descent down the slopes and into the clouds below, leaving the Hammer-Heads to argue among themselves.

For several agonizingly long minutes, the Magic Picture showed only haze and clouds as the lone figure descended into Oz.

By now, Dorothy and the others had joined Princess Ozma and Glinda as they all waited for the mist to clear.

"What a silly looking creature that was," the Cowardly Lion exclaimed.

Everyone agreed that the creature on the stairway was very unique.

"I thought it was a person, like myself," Dorothy observed. "But its head looked kinda odd."

"And that hair!" exclaimed the Cowardly Lion. "I wonder if he had a perm?"

Once more, everyone agreed.

Just then, the mist surrounding the lone figure on the descending stairway parted and the lone figure, shovel in hand, thrust his arms high into the air in a show of victory.

If Dorothy thought the lone figure looked "kinda odd" before, she was certain of it now.

The Magic Picture now focused on the lone figure, whose head now resembled a giant peach. Oddly enough, the copper-blond hair still remained and looked more alive than the Giant Peach it was now sitting on top of.

Princess Ozma furrowed Her brow as the creature waved and winked at various shadows now surrounding it.

"Its head turned into a Giant Peach on the way down, didn't it?" Glinda asked the gathering, all of whom agreed that the creature had resembled a man at the top and was now a creature with a Giant Peach for a head.

They all looked at the retired Wizard of Oz, who only shrugged his shoulders. He was thoroughly stumped as to how this stranger had made his way into Oz and come upon a set of Magic Stairs.

"Strange magic indeed..." Princess Ozma mused out loud.

The Scarecrow shook his head and scratched his brow. "Something doesn't add up," he said.

"But it was a grandiose entrance, wasn't it?" asked the Tin Woodman.

Chapter 3
"My Beautiful General"

For several minutes, the lone figure stood alone at the bottom of the Magic Staircase, looking about and admiring his many fans and admirers with great admiration. The winds howled his praises and the shadows cheered him on as the lone figure pondered his next move.

Just then, a sudden noise caught his attention and the lone figure looked down upon what appeared to be a common metal trash can.

He poked it with the shovel, then lifted the lid from the gray receptacle and immediately noticed an eye looking directly up at him.

"Goodness gracious!" he shouted. "Why, it's a commoner... and I do so love the uneducated!"

The lone figure reached out and retrieved from the trash can an object that appeared more like a crumpled piece of newspaper than an actual living creature.

With a flourish of his tiny hands, the lone figure shook the crumpled piece of newspaper like a towel in the wind until it became a creature whose appearance was as strange and unexpected as the lone figure.

"Greetings great friend!" exclaimed the newly released creature. "My name is General Blug, though I'm not sure of my rank anymore. Thank you for freeing me from being thrown away."

"A General, you say?" inquired the lone figure. His brow furrowed but for a moment when a thought crossed his mind.

For several minutes, General Blug spoke of this and that… and even some of the other.

General Blug had, in years past, served the Nome King as the General of his armies, commanding more than forty nine thousand, nine hundred and ninety nine well-drilled Nomes in the Art of War.

His only mistake was having argued against the Nome King's plan to overthrow Princess Ozma, forcing his own removal by means of being "thrown away", which was in this case a metal trash can.

"You say that the Nome King knocked you out with His sapphire scepter?" the lone figure inquired.

"Indeed he did," replied General Blug, "and then he had me thrown away."

The lone figure looked General Blug over, pondering what he might gain from this creature that clearly looked like it had been in a trash can for well over a hundred years.

Once more, the thought crossed his mind and the lone figure stood erect, puffed out his chest and pouted ponderously as he stared intently. He then handed the creature the shovel.

"Carry my shovel and you shall be my Beautiful General!" the lone figure exclaimed. "And I shall be your Trump!!"

Chapter 4
Rumors

For the next several days, all anyone could talk about was the odd-looking stranger who had appeared in Quadling Country. Once word got out beyond Emerald City, the lone figure was the center of attention throughout the Land of Oz.

There were rumors swirling about that the lone figure was called The Trump, while others swore that his hair was actually a living creature and companion to the lone figure. Some even suggested that the lone figure was King Pastoria Himself, returned from the Great Beyond.

"I hear tell that the creature down in Quadling Country is nothing more than a giant peach that's been made alive by the Powder of Life," the Munchkin farmer confided to his Gillikin cousin, who had been visiting from the north.

"Naw! You're just Twattling... That's all," replied the Gillikin Cousin. "Nothing more than idle gossip."

Several Winkies gathered in the blacksmith shop of the Castle of the Tin Woodman and remarked about the Nome travelling with The Trump.

"Are you sure it's called 'The Trump'? And what about that Nome travelling with it?" the Winkie blacksmith asked his closest friends gathered around the anvil.

"I heard the Nome was Roquat the Red in disguise as Ruggedo... though any Nome King will do in a pinch," the blacksmith's friend replied.

"It's ten feet tall and smells like peaches," a young Quadling girl whispered to her sister. "And it shouts 'Fee Fi Fo Fum!'"

The two sisters giggled as they ran out into their yard to play.

"I wonder why this creature has come to Oz," Dorothy mused softly to her friend, Princess Ozma.

The Royal Ruler of Oz furrowed Her brow and pondered the situation of the newcomer. "This one is different," She remarked coolly. "We must figure out its name and purpose before it figures out ours."

Chapter 5
China Country

For the next several days, the lone figure and the General slowly made their way westward along the road of red brick which ran throughout the Quadling Country.

Along the way, they encountered various locals, all of whom seemed to have already heard of them. This fact caused great pleasure for the lone figure, who confirmed to a local farmer that he was The Trump. There were also countless offers of food, drink and lodging, all of which slowed them down immensely.

The Trump, it seems, had a fear of what he called "germs", which General Blug could not quite understand. As such, the needs of the lone figure were constant and quite demanding as he navigated the fears and musings that came forth from The Trump. He soon discovered that it helped immensely if he spoke the name 'The Trump' in as many sentences as he could, and always complimentary.

In time, The Trump and General Blug came upon a signpost pointing towards a winding spur of red brick, leading towards the south. Overhead, a faint rainbow crossed the sky.

"China Country!" The Trump declared as he read the signpost.

"If we keep stopping, we'll never get anywhere!" General Blug exclaimed. "We could have been somewhere by now."

"You don't understand my Beautiful General. I have to appease these common folks by making them think that I'm one of them. That way, they'll do anything I say without question," The Trump explained.

The look on General Blug's face was one of confusion and The Trump continued on.

"Common folks are a stupid lot indeed. You pay them a simple compliment and claim to understand their plight and they'll follow you anywhere. A lie here and a lie there and before you know it, they're hooked," he said plainly.

"So you do understand their lives?" the confused General asked.

The Trump snorted with laughter.

"Of course not! These people are beneath me," The Trump replied. "I have more money than anyone around here because I am the greatest businessman that ever lived!"

"Money? Money has little value here and is more of curiosity than anything," General Blug countered. "At least it used to be."

"Nonsense!" The Trump shouted. "Money is everything! Clearly, you don't understand!"

The Trump started down the path towards China Country with General Blug following close behind.

The General started to explain the nature of China Country when The Trump interrupted him.

"I know all about China, General Blug!" The Trump exclaimed. "In fact, I clearly know more than you'll ever know about everything. They'll be no trouble at all. We just declare a trade war and wait them out!"

"What is a trade war?" General Blug inquired.

"You wouldn't understand, my Beautiful General. Only I can fully understand what needs to be done. Why, only I can solve whatever problems arise between China and us!" The Trump droned on.

For the next few minutes, The Trump extolled his own virtues regarding war and peace and all things in between. It seems that The Trump was convinced that he was the greatest thing since sliced bread.

"What's so great about sliced bread?" General Blug tried asking The Trump, who had already moved on to the virtues of the expansive Great Wall of China which stretched out before them and surrounded the entire China Country.

The Trump looked over as much of the wall as he could see and noticed that there was no gate.

General Blug walked up to the wall, tapped it gently with his toe and looked over at The Trump.

"Not so great a wall after all, is it?" The Trump said scornfully. He then trod over to the china wall and kicked it with the heel of his shoe.

"Good thing I don't have bone spurs," The Trump thought to himself.

All at once, a crack formed, which quickly grew in size as it snaked its way up the white china wall.

Moments later, pieces of white china porcelain began tumbling down from the wall until a sizable hole appeared.

"You have broken their wall, my Trump!" General Blug exclaimed.

The Trump walked through the hole, looked back and snickered. "No worry there, my Beautiful General. I'll pay half the amount it takes to rebuild it and make them sue me for the rest. Besides, I can blame it all on those knuckleheads I escaped from back there and make them pay for it!" he declared while pointing southward at the nearby mountain where he had descended the Magic Stairs.

"What does 'sue me' mean?" General Blug thought to himself as he stepped through the hole in the wall.

It only took several strides before The Trump and his Beautiful General were overwhelmed by the beauty and majesty of China Country.

The floor of China Country was polished porcelain of the finest quality The Trump had ever seen. Before him were houses of all manner and each, made of the finest porcelain Oz has to offer.

"Everything is so tiny," General Blug observed as he pointed out the china trees and streams and even the small mountains off in the distance.

The Trump was impressed by the majesty of the porcelain country and pondered several thoughts regarding their wealth and status.

As The Trump stood there, flanked by General Blug, the local inhabitants began to emerge from their houses and such, curious about the arrival of the very tall newcomers. They were particularly fascinated by the taller one, who's head looked like a giant peach.

The citizens of China Country were a curious assortment of figures, all made of china porcelain and living in every way one would imagine.

There were nobility classes, which includes Kings, Queens, Princesses and Dukes, as well as commoners and elites. In fact, all manner of classes and nobility were represented within the confines of China Country. There was even a clown, though The Trump found the repaired cracks from his many pratfalls disturbing and repellant.

"Looks like the kinda ugly scars you'd find on an immigrant," The Trump mused loudly towards the clown, whose happy face now wore a frown.

General Blug looked down upon the gathered citizenry of China Country with great interest. They were only as tall as his waist and were greatly fearful of what harm a creature of his stature could do to them.

At once, a nearby band began a somber melody of grandeur as several porcelain figures of nobility approached.

"They look like chess pieces," The Trump thought to himself. *"Better avoid them and find the uneducated."*

The Trump trod roughly across the fine porcelain floor of China Country in search of the countryside and left behind a trail of broken and cracked china. The sound of breaking china alone was deafening to the local populace, and there were moans and complaints about the damage the tall stranger was causing.

General Blug stood firm in his place at the cracked china wall and watched as The Trump wrecked havoc just by walking about China Country. The Beautiful General looked up and noticed a small dark cloud roll in from outside. The cloud slowed down until it was hovering just over the center of the town where everyone had gathered, seeking shelter from the menace of The Trump.

For several moments, as The Trump grew bored and headed back to where General Blug was standing firm, the small cloud grew, and grew… and grew even more, until the horizon of China Country was entirely covered in clouds.

"Let's blow this joint!" The Trump exclaimed, gesturing to his Beautiful General that they should beat a hasty retreat.

As The Trump and General Blug turned to step back through the cracked opening of the china wall, the clouds above let loose with a torrent of snow and hail and several bolts of lightning, resulting in various screams and such from the local populace.

The Trump turned back around and laughed loudly.

"There's your Global Warming!!!" he proclaimed. "Tell you what. I'll send my fixer to fix it all for you. It'll be a Great Wall, you'll see. Those knuckleheads over there will pay for it!" He pointed through the crack in the china wall at the distant mountain peak to the east.

Just then, a small and very dainty china resident, clearly of noble class, approached The Trump and shouted up at him.

"I am the Countess Von Noritake and I demand that you explain yourself and what you intend to do about the mess you've left behind!!" the dainty china Countess declared.

The Trump looked down on the Countess Von Noritake and a smile crossed his thin, pasty lips. He reached down and grabbed the Countess very roughly and brought her close to his face.

Before the Countess could even protest, The Trump planted a very sloppy kiss upon the very dainty noble-class lady. He then set the Countess down upon the porcelain floor of China Country, whereupon she fell into several broken pieces, having succumbed to The Trump's fumbling tiny hands.

The Countess Von Noritake looked up, only to see the back of The Trump as he made his way through the cracked wall of china and back into Quadling Country. She was unable to shout out or even lodge a feeble protest, given her broken condition.

General Blug watched it all in silence and looked down upon the Countess with subdued pity. He turned and followed his Trump out of China Country and back to Quadling Country.

Chapter 6
Climate Change

Back from her visit with Princess Ozma and Dorothy, Glinda; Good Witch of the South read purposefully as the Great Book of Records spelled out The Trump's misadventure in China Country. She was stunned to find her spell over the China Country wall broken by the creature with the head of a giant peach. The spell she had placed on the wall long ago had kept out any foul weather, be it rain, lightning, hail or snow.

Now, China Country was at the mercy of Mother Nature, who was no fan of walls.

Glinda called for a nearby Handmaiden, who approached quickly and curtsied.

"Fetch me my broomstick please," the Good Witch of the South said politely.

With that, the Handmaiden was off in a flash. Moments later, she returned with a long-handled broomstick.

The broomstick itself was fashioned from a fallen branch of a hickory tree, which Glinda had attached a small sheave of straw by means of a stout length of twine. She had then enchanted it with a Jackdaw feather.

It had been a few years after the demise of both Wicked Witches at the hands of Dorothy Gale of Kansas when Glinda had decided to give riding a broomstick a try.

"After all, I am a witch… and why should the wicked ones have all the fun?" Glinda often thought to herself.

Of course, it was immense fun for the Good Witch of the South, but her sojourns into the skies above Quadling Country made the local Quadlings a bit nervous. It seems that the Quadlings never lost their fear of flying witches, so Glinda would confine her flights to nighttime flights or in extreme emergency.

Today, it appeared, was an extreme emergency.

In no time, Glinda was airborne and headed northwest directly over the Mountain of the Hammerheads and westward towards China Country. She looked down to see a band of Hammerheads staring up at her and shouting. Glinda waved politely and began searching the western horizon for China Country.

It wasn't hard for Glinda to locate China Country at all as it was covered entirely by a large, black cloud which would explode occasionally with flashes of lightning and booms of thunder.

After a quick landing by the large crack in the wall, Glinda found herself confronted with a storm, the likes of which she had never encountered before. The intensity of it all was overwhelming and she thought she could hear the screams of the local inhabitants inside.

The Good Witch of the South retrieved her Magic Wand from a long thin pouch attached to her bodice.

"I call upon the Water Nymphs to take away the water from above," Glinda exclaimed as she waved her Magic Wand high above her head.

Moments later, a covey of Water Nymphs, sent by Polychrome herself descended from the heavens and surrounded the black cloud. In a matter of moments, the Water Nymphs had dissipated the entire storm, with only a bucket of water to show for their efforts.

Glinda watched with great joy as the blue skies of Oz reappeared over China Country. A gentle wave of her Magic Wand and the wall surrounding China Country was made whole once more.

The Ruler of the Quadling Country made her way through the village and repaired what needed it and comforted those in need, which was practically everyone.

Glinda soon came upon the clown, who was still frowning and sitting alone in the town square.

"Are you okay?" She asked the frowning china clown.

"No Mam," he replied. "That thing called me ugly because of my cracks."

Glinda turned away briefly to wipe away a tear, then composed herself and knelt down to comfort the clown.

"Would you like me to enchant your cracks away and make you look normal?" she asked gently.

The clown thought for a moment, then a look of resolve took over his face.

"No Mam. My cracks and repairs are who I am... and I like who I am," the now-smiling clown replied.

Glinda; Good Witch of the South and Ruler of the Quadling Country nodded knowingly and leaned over to kiss the clown most gently upon his forehead, causing the clown to blush slightly. Like everyone else in Quadling Country, he knew that Glinda's kiss was a sign of her protection and he felt an overwhelming sense of humility and Love.

"Truer words have never been spoken," she proclaimed softly. "You have wisdom beyond measure."

Glinda now made her way back towards the village. The sound of rustling china nearby caught her attention and she ventured over towards an overturned broken teacup.

"My Goodness!" Glinda exclaimed as she came upon Princess Von Noritake, who was in many pieces and not quite herself as she peeked out from the broken part of the teacup.

"Please pardon my appearance Glinda," the Princess spoke apologetically. "It was that thing with a gigantic peach for a head. Its hair seemed almost alive."

Glinda shuddered as she brushed away the remains of the broken teacup. The Good Witch of the

South waved her Magic Wand over the numerous pieces gathered about the upper part of Princess Von Noritake.

In a brilliant flash of green light and only a small wisp of green smoke, Princess Von Noritake was made whole as well.

It took Glinda; Good Witch of the South and Ruler of Quadling Country over an hour to get the Princess to calm down, the violence of her assault by the creature having overwhelmed the nobility of the Noritake.

"You say the other creature was a Nome and he only followed?" Glinda asked curiously.

All the Princess could do was nod in agreement.

Nomes it seems are solitary creatures, whose interaction with others usually goes wrong at some point.

Glinda felt a twinge of concern and was pondering the possibility that something was wrong.

"Which way did the creatures go?" Glinda asked in a very soft tone.

By now, Princess Von Noritake had calmed down enough to point towards the west.

Chapter 7
Bullshit!

The Trump and General Blug continued on their way westward, leaving China Country in shambles behind them.

The Beautiful General, for his part, was grateful that they were back on the road. The look on Princess Von Noritake's face was stuck in his mind and he did not like it one bit. He also noticed that the shovel he had been carrying on his back seemed to be getting heavier by the mile.

Once more, local folks began gathering around The Trump as they made their way along the road of red brick. They pressed him for answers regarding the ominous clouds hovering low over China Country. The Trump was more than happy to oblige and launched into a rather lengthy tirade.

"My friends, my peons, my uneducated! China was attacked by those knuckle-heads over there!" he shouted while pointing back behind him at the ominous clouds looming over the horizon. The large peach-headed creature droned on and on about something to do with climate change, which none of the locals gathered about had any inkling of. "They tore down the wall and brought it upon themselves! They're the ones who should be paying to rebuild the wall. And it'll be a beautiful wall, with spikes and nails..."

"And puppy dog tails, I suppose?" questioned a skeptic in the audience.

Everyone laughed, though only about half or so got it.

"At least they'll pay for it… I guarantee it!!!" The Trump exclaimed.

General Blug, who had taken a quiet posture while the creature with the head of peach preached on and on about something to do with this or that… or something other, watched as The Trump's hair slowly became animated. The old Nome stood transfixed as the hair on top of the spewing peach head took on a life of its own.

Oddly enough, none of the gathered locals noticed the oddly-behaving hair as nearly half the audience fawned over every word the peach spoke while the other half of them watched in stunned silence.

"My tax records are none of anyone's business but my own, though they're perfect… and beautiful, and I don't know how you people tolerate the bullshit that vomits from that green glow over there…" The Trump bellowed loudly across the landscape.

There was yet another stunned silence as everyone struggled to comprehend the new word that had issued from the peach's lips.

The lesser half of the assembled masses started pushing the greater half around, which in turn made the pushed half push back, until a full-on scrum had occurred.

The Trump backed off and watched gleefully as everyone fought over its newest tactic.

"What is… bullshit?" The Beautiful General inquired of The Trump.

"That's called a diversion," The Trump whispered behind his hand.

Just then, both sides of the scrum separated and began chanting "bullshit" at each other in rapid succession.

Chapter 8
Cockwomble

The Trump and General Blug separated themselves from the angry mob and strolled swiftly away towards the west and past a sign that read…

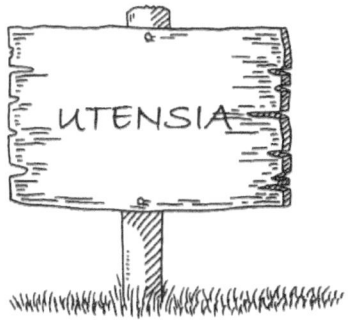

"Aren't we going to stop and harass this place?" General Blug inquired.

The Trump looked down the old path that led southward.

"Na! Probably just another shithole country," the peach declared.

The old Nome was taken aback once more. Now there were two new words which he didn't understand.

The two of them continued westward through the reddish countryside of Quadling Country.

After a time, when the chanting behind them had subsided, more due to distance than enthusiasm, did the old Nome finally speak up.

"You did that on purpose," he said deliberately. "But why?"

"I told you before… Diversion!" The Trump declared.

Before the Beautiful General could answer, a blur passed between the two, barely heard and even more barely seen.

"I heard that and I saw what you did…" the blur said softly as it passed once more between the two travelers.

The Trump became enraged and demanded to know who, what, where and most importantly… how the blur had found out. He noticed that it seemed a bit brighter and clearer as it slowly passed by him. He could also now see that the ethereal creature appeared to be a female of extraordinary beauty and grace.

Her gown, which seemed almost like a gentle fluffy cloud, was streaked with the colors of the rainbow and her long hair resembled a soft cool flame waving in the breeze.

"You're nothing but scum, and you can't prove a thing! In fact, I'll sue you so fast it'll make your little girl head spin!" the giant peach head spouted. "You hear me?!"

General Blug watched silently as the peach berated the ethereal creature standing before them.

Once again, The Trump's hair became animated and even more agitated than before.

Finally, when the peach had stopped yelling for a moment to catch its breath did the ethereal creature speak.

"You sir, are a Cockwomble," she said softly. The creature danced about, twirling daintily and giggling as she did so.

The hair on top of the peach's head grew larger as it puffed itself up.

"And just what is a Cockwomble?!" The Trump demanded of General Blug.

The old Nome chuckled to himself, recalling his days serving Roquat, the Nome King. His behavior reminded General Blug of the creature now standing before him, who was glaring at the ethereal creature.

"She's saying that you are making outrageously stupid statements and acting like a child while thinking you're the greatest thing in Oz," General Blug explained.

"Of course I'm the greatest! Haven't you figured that out by now?!!!" The Trump declared. "I'm getting really tired of having to explain the obvious to you, General!"

It was clear to the Beautiful General that The Trump had only heard what it wanted to hear. He shook his head in disbelief and noticed that the shovel had grown heavier in the last few minutes.

41

"You sir, are not worth my time," the ethereal creature spoke softly as she turned towards the rapidly approaching rainbow.

"Why you snotty little bitch! Don't you know who I am?!" The Trump demanded.

General Blug watched once more as The Trump's hair grew agitated and began waving about as though it too were quite angry.

The ethereal creature giggled softly as she danced and whirled about. The rainbow now stopped before her and she was carried aloft onto the soft yet vibrant colors and slowly vanished into the clouds above.

"I should 'a known," The Trump mused aloud.

"Known what?" General Blug replied.

"She's one of those rainbow cunts... probably a fucking lesbian!" The Trump spouted. "Bitches like that always are! It's a waste of perfectly good meat!"

The old Nome just shook his head in confusion. The creature that had saved him from the trash bin kept spewing new words he didn't understand, but he was fairly certain he didn't want to know.

Just then, the mound of hair that had been quite agitated reached out and slapped General Blug hard on the head.

Chapter 9
Que Veritas?

The Trump gazed out over the vast countryside and moaned loudly.

"There's gotta be a better way to travel in this place!" he declared. "We've been walking for days and it's getting' old! Aren't there any golf carts in this place?!"

General Blug remained silent, as he had for most of the journey so far. A nagging feeling had appeared in his mind early on and now it was growing.

"There!" The Trump declared as he pointed northward towards the green glow of Emerald City. "What is that all about?"

The Beautiful General hesitated for a moment as he recalled the long walk of the last few days. A glimmer of hope sparkled but for a moment, then was consumed by darkness.

"That is the Emerald City I spoke to you of yesterday, and the day before, when you asked about a capital," General Blug said. "Princess Ozma? Remember?"

The Trump didn't miss a beat in his reply.

"Ahhh, yes. That was a great idea of mine. We'll go to Emerald City where I shall become King! I'll be the greatest King ever! It'll be beautiful!!"

General Blug gave The Trump a puzzled look. He didn't recall The Trump ever discussing the conquest of Emerald City. He once more thought back to his days of old when he commanded armies for the Nome King, Roquat of the Rocks.

Memories of plots and intrigue and his expulsion from power into a trash can rushed through his mind as The Trump raved on and on about things he clearly didn't understand.

Before General Blug could utter a response, The Trump was in his face and pointing a tiny finger at him.

"I'm gonna let you in on a little secret, my Beautiful General," The Trump whispered softly.

General Blug looked around. To his amazement, they were utterly alone. For several days, crowds had been their constant companion. But now, no one was in sight as The Trump whispered his secret.

"Everything I say is a lie," he confided to the astonished Nome. "After all, what is truth? It's just an inconvenience."

"Que Veritas…" the Beautiful General whispered back, recalling the words of the Nome King one day when

he had argued his plans for conquest of Princess Ozma.
"What is truth?"

Chapter 10
Polychrome's Advice

Glinda looked up and saw a brilliant splash of color. She smiled broadly as the ethereal creature came floating down from the brilliant rainbow that had landed before her.

"Polychrome. How wonderful to see you again," said Glinda. She approached the softly glowing creature, who looked somewhat like a dainty girl, but was in fact a Sky Fairy and Daughter of the Great Rainbow.

Polychrome danced about, cheerful and full of joy as Glinda watched.

In time, Polychrome came to rest and smiled softly at the Good Witch of the South.

"I've just met a most vile and disgusting creature," she said matter-of-factly. "Head like a peach and the oddest hair. It's foul, loathsome and most dishonest."

Glinda pursed her lips and shook her head.

"Tell me more, please," she said.

Polychrome spoke for some time regarding her meeting with the loathsome creature she had met just beyond the western horizon past Utensia.

"It seems to delight in using very ugly language," she informed Glinda, who listened intently. "I called it a Cockwomble."

Glinda chuckled softly. She knew what a Cockwomble was and wondered what this new creature was like.

"You mentioned its hair being odd?" Glinda inquired. "Are you certain of that?"

Polychrome danced about as she pondered her response.

"It is a living creature who feeds on fear and anger and vomits evil," Polychrome said softly. "Be wary of it, for it controls the peach below."

49

In that moment, Polychrome nodded happily as the Great Rainbow passed slowly by, collecting his daughter and making for the north.

In no time at all, Glinda found herself alone and pondering the strange creature and its hair. She mounted her broomstick and took off, heading westward.

The Good Witch of the South looked down to see various crowds of people along the road of red brick, all of whom seemed to be shouting at each other.

After a few more minutes of flight, Rigmarole Town came into view, Glinda saw two figures standing alone on the road of red brick.

Chapter 11
A Handful of Glinda

The wind rushed through Glinda's hair as she swooped down from above and executed a perfect three-point landing directly in front of the creature with the head of a peach, and an old Nome.

Dismounting her broom, Glinda looked about before settling her gaze upon the peach.

"You were fairly easy to find," she said matter-of-factly. "All I had to do was follow the mayhem."

Without missing a beat, the peach launched into what the old Nome had learned was a well rehearsed routine.

"What? That mayhem was 'cause of them knuckleheads over there," the peach said while pointing at the fairly distant mountains to the southeast.

It continued on for several minutes, blaming everything but itself as the peach sought to deflect attention from itself.

Before Glinda could utter a response, the peach came forward and spoke softly.

"Look Toots, don't worry about it. I know more about stuff than your pretty little head could ever hold," it said. "Most folks call me The Trump, but you can call me Don."

The Trump reached out and placed his arm around her shoulders while reaching forth with his opposing hand and grabbing Glinda by the breast. He gave a rough squeeze before letting go and reaching down between Glinda's thighs and grabbing hard. At the same time, he planted a sloppy wet kiss on her lips.

"What's your name, sweetie?" The Trump asked as he disengaged from the Good Witch of the South.

"Goodness gracious!" Glinda exclaimed. She reached beneath her bodice and retrieved her Magic Wand, which appeared to come out of nowhere.

With a strong swing, Glinda connected solidly with The Trump's head, causing a large shower of bright green sparks.

The Trump stood there, stunned and speechless while the Beautiful General looked on in amazement.

Glinda backed off a bit as the peach shook itself back to reality.

The Trump looked to his subordinate with disdain and the hair clinging to the top of the peach once more took on a Life of its own, snarling at General Blug and Glinda.

"Polychrome was wrong about you," the Good Witch of the South observed. "You're not so much a Cockwomble. You're more a very small creature with a very high opinion… of yourself."

Once more, General Blug found himself trying to stifle a laugh. He knew once more what the magical creatures of Oz already knew well. The Trump had no clue what truth was. The hair was another thing indeed.

"What is she on about?" The Trump inquired.

"She is calling you a Cockalorum… if I understand the term correctly. I'm not in the habit of being fluent in the speak of the Up-Stairs People… and I had been a long time in that trash can, so my language skills are…" General Blug replied. He shrugged his shoulders and The Trump produced what the old Nome thought to be a smile, which he had not seen the peach do before.

"Why are all these broads talking about my cock?!" The Trump bellowed. He strutted about and tried to approach Glinda once more.

The Good Witch of the South and Sovereign Ruler of the Quadling Country, now aware of the creature's ways, shoved her magic wand directly into the chest of The Trump.

Once more, a shower of green sparks stopped him in his tracks.

"There'll be no more of that!" she declared.

Glinda mounted her broomstick and pointed her finger at the highly agitated hair atop the peach.

"We'll be back for you when we've figured out what you are!" Glinda said confidently.

The Trump and the Beautiful General stood there, transfixed as Glinda flew off in a blaze of red smoke.

General Blug inhaled deeply as he recognized the smell of burning ruby crystals from long ago.

A memory returned and the old Nome remembered days of old when he commanded legions.

Chapter 12
Next!

It didn't take long for The Trump to lose interest in whatever it was that had just happened and now turned his attention to the countryside in search of admirers and the newest thing.

General Blug remained speechless as his mind raced with thoughts of honor among Nomes. To all Nomes, Up-Stairs People are anyone who lives above ground and they were normally to be avoided. Like all Nomes, he preferred the solitude of his own domain beneath the rock and soil of the land and rarely chose to associate with Up-Stairs People... and now the old Nome remembered why.

By now, the shovel had not only grown unbearably heavy, but now felt hot as molten rock.

The General grabbed the shovel from an improvised holster he had fashioned just after receiving it. He threw it down hard, where it impaled the ground and stood nearly straight up.

"I may have been thrown away for what seems like a century or more, but even I know who that was you just violated!" the old Nome proclaimed. He was very angry and The Trump looked perplexed. The hair had assumed a pose and remained very still.

"Whaaat?" The Trump said. "Is that broad someone? She rich? Something like that? What gives?"

"That was Glinda; Good Witch of the South and..."

The Trump interrupted, as he always did with everyone he met, and corrected his Beautiful General.

"Did you say bitch?" The Trump asked excitedly. "I should 'a known. She's the wicked bitch of the west!"

General Blug watched as The Trump danced about and sang some odd song about a wicked bitch being dead.

In that moment, something in the old Nome's mind snapped and he shook his head to clear his thoughts. He looked at The Trump and came to a sudden realization that he was looking at the reincarnation of Ruggedo, the old Nome King who ruled long ago. He also understood that this one was worse by a large margin.

"That's it!" General Blug shouted. I'm done with you!"

"Whaaat? What's with you and the broad? Hell, she loved it. They all do. I can do anything I want with them. You see me grab her pussy?!"

He laughed loudly as the General turned to walk away.

Hey! Wait!" The Trump shouted.

General Blug turned around and watched as the hair on top of the peach stretched itself out and grabbed the upright shovel.

Before the old Nome could react, the hair swung the shovel hard and connected against the General's head.

The old Nome collapsed in a split-second back into a crumpled wad, much like The Trump had found him. He landed a few yards away in the middle of the road of red brick.

Just then, an old wagon came rumbling down the road, driven by an old man and pulled by one of the local zebras who lived nearby.

The Trump watched as the wagon passed directly over the crumpled wad of his Beautiful General. He chuckled as General Blug became lodged beneath the rumbling wagon and was carried away into the distance.

"Next!" shouted The Trump as he turned westward towards a sign that read:

Rigmarole
Town

Chapter 13
MOGA

Following the grandiose entrance of the creature with the head of a peach, the Tin Woodman returned to his Tin Palace in Winkie Country where he had served as Emperor of the Winkies for over a hundred years now.

For the next few days, word trickled in from various travelers of a creature traveling across the Quadling Country, calling itself The Trump. It travelled with an old Nome; and while some called The Trump the greatest creature since the Wizard of Oz, others decried it as the worst creature since the Wicked Witch of the East… or West.

"What do you think of this creature called The Trump?" the Tin Woodman asked his friend Jack Pumpkinhead, who had dropped by the Tin Palace for a visit.

"I really couldn't say," he replied. "What little I've heard from people passing by my place doesn't make any sense."

He scratched the small stem that protruded from the top of his pumpkin head.

"Someone told me it saved China Country from a horrible disaster, while another said it was the cause of the disaster," Jack continued. "I've even been told it wants to march on Emerald City and save everyone from Princess Ozma."

"Why would anyone want to depose Princess Ozma? She's the most wonderful ruler anyone could ever ask for," asked the Tin Woodman. He placed his hand upon the small nickel-plated door that covered his heart; a gift from the Wizard of Oz of a silken heart stuffed with sawdust. "Why, Her heart is even bigger and more loving than mine."

Jack Pumpkinhead, who was nothing more than a collection of wood branches and a hand-carved pumpkin, cobbled together and brought to Life by the Powder of Life, shrugged his arms in disbelief.

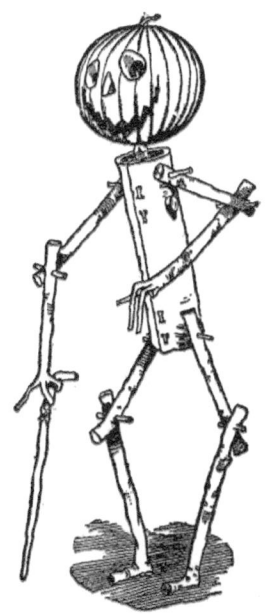

"I dunno," he replied.

The Tin Woodman, whose official title was **Emperor Nicholas III of the House of Chopper**, sat upon his tin throne in deep thought as he pondered the mystery of The Trump.

After a time, he had come to a decision.

"I must seek this creature out and meet it. Perhaps determine who or what it is and what its intentions are," the Emperor declared.

He immediately set out in search of The Trump.

By the following morning, the Tin Woodman had already crossed the Winkie River and made his way into Quadling Country by way of the road of red brick, which ran through the southern part of the land.

Along the way, he encountered numerous locals who passed along rumors and hearsay about the creature called The Trump and its companion, an old Nome called the Beautiful General.

As he walked briskly along the road of red brick, the Tin Woodman came across an odd sign he had never seen before.

Make
Oz
Great
Again!

"What a peculiar sign," he mused to himself. "The Land of Oz has always been great. Why would it need to be made great again?"

Still puzzling over the odd sign as he once more made his way eastward, Emperor Nicholas III of the House of Chopper came across a local Quadling, who seemed quite agitated.

"What troubles you, kind sir?" the Tin Woodman asked.

"There's a lunatic running around the countryside shouting and screaming about pure nonsense!" the local exclaimed.

The Tin Woodman stood silently as the old man ranted and raved about some creature called The Trump. He spoke about outlandish promises and bizarre claims that made no sense to him.

"What does bullshit mean?" he asked the Tin Woodman.

Emperor Nicholas III of the House of Chopper shrugged his shiny, nickel-plated shoulders.

"Well, he kept saying that word… and now everyone's saying it!" the Quadling shouted. "Bullshit this and bullshit that! Nonsense, I tell you!!!"

"Where did you see this creature?" the Tin Woodman asked.

The Quadling pointed towards the signpost by the small cobblestone road that lead southward.

"The last I saw of him, he was headed towards Rigmarole Town," he said.

Chapter 14
Politicians

     Glinda; Good Witch of the South and Ruler of the Quadling Country circled the Emerald City twice before setting down by the Forbidden Fountain and making her way into Princess Ozma's Palace. She was clearly agitated, which was unusual for her as Glinda was known throughout the Land of Oz for her calm and pleasant demeanor.

     Princess Ozma watched from Her perch within the Royal Palace Gardens as Glinda came swiftly through the abundant vegetation to Her royal branch.

"Oh Glinda! I watched as that creature attacked you. It was all so fast and…" the Princess whispered. "I'm so sorry…"

Despite looking younger, Princess Ozma was, in fact, many years older, though how many is unknown. She is, by definition a fairy, and therefore immortal.

Glinda, on the other hand, is a witch. Despite that fact, she too is immortal, though considerably younger than Ozma.

Nonetheless, neither had ever encountered a creature such as The Trump before.

"The creature we should fear is the one that resides upon the top of the peach," Glinda explained. "That is the one in power, not the peach or the body it is attached to."

"But it assaulted you in a most vile and disgusting way," Princess Ozma replied. "That I cannot tolerate."

For an hour or more, Glinda and Ozma went back and forth about The Trump. Princess Ozma explained the fate of the old Nome.

"Threw him under the wagon, you say?" Glinda inquired.

"Indeed… "Princess Ozma replied. "General Blug did not a Beautiful General make."

"What about Dorothy?" Glinda asked.

Princess Ozma confirmed that Dorothy had witnessed the assault on Glinda by the Giant Peach with Her.

"The Magic Picture was quite clear and focused and Dorothy became very upset… and very angry," Princess Ozma explained. "We've been watching this creature for days. It's from the Great Outside and is like nothing Oz has ever seen before."

Glinda confessed her horror at finding China Country in ruins and her dismay regarding the local populace along the road of red brick.

"There is a new word spreading around the land," Glinda announced calmly. "It is a most unpleasant and vulgar word."

"We've heard it even here in the Royal Court. I do believe it's pronounced 'Bullshit'," Princess Ozma replied.

Glinda nodded in agreement while Princess Ozma pondered the situation. In short time, an idea made itself known to Her.

Princess Ozma called for a Servant Girl, who promptly appeared, took whispered instructions, and just as quickly vanished to perform her errand.

A scant few minutes later and an older couple appeared within the Royal Court.

"Welcome Aunt Em and Uncle Henry!" Princess Ozma declared. "Thank you so kindly for attending me on such short notice." She recalled the stories Dorothy had told Her long ago about life in Kansas and smiled sweetly at the old couple.

The old couple blushed and bowed humbly before the Royal Monarch. They had lived in Oz for over a hundred years, brought there at the request of Dorothy when she chose to live in the Land of Oz long ago. Even so, the old habits of Kansas remained and were one of their most endearing qualities.

"What 'kin we do you 'fer?" Uncle Henry inquired.

"Have you heard about this creature called The Trump?" the Royal Ruler of Oz asked.

"Yes, we have. It's all anyone is talking about!" Aunt Em exclaimed.

Princess Ozma and Glinda spent the next hour explaining to the old couple the activities of The Trump while they nodded and listened carefully.

"Sounds to me like you gots you one of them thar' politicians," Uncle Henry suggested.

Aunt Em nodded vigorously in agreement. "Yes mam! That's one of them ther' politicians! No doubt about it."

Princess Ozma called for the Magic Picture, which arrived almost immediately.

Moments later, the Magic Picture showed the creature heading down the cobblestone pathway leading towards Rigmarole Town.

"Goodness!" Princess Ozma exclaimed. "It's headed for the Defensive Settlements."

"The Rigmaroles won't stand a chance," Glinda suggested, "though I'm more worried for the Flutterbudgets."

Minutes later, Princess Ozma smiled as She watched the Tin Woodman make his way down the cobblestone pathway towards the small village.

Princess Ozma turned towards the old couple. "You say it's a politician?"

For the next half hour or so, Uncle Henry and Aunt Em returned the favor and described all manner of politicians they had heard about during their life in Kansas.

"And how do you deal with them?" Glinda asked.

"The only way to git' rid of 'em is to vote 'em out!" Uncle Henry exclaimed.

Aunt Em nodded vigorously in agreement.

Chapter 15
The Rigmaroles

In the Quadling Country of Oz, near the border of Winkie Country are two distinct defensive settlements; Rigmarole Town and Flutterbudget Center. They are defensive settlements due to the nature of the citizenry contained within each settlement.

The Rigmaroles find comfort and security in the rituals of long-winded speeches designed to pass along virtually no useful information.

They often compete for the most long-winded speech, extemporaneous speaking and even name-dropping under bizarre circumstances.

Virtually every action of the day, be it breakfast, gathering fruit or doing laundry, required a long, drawn-out speech. As such, very little got done while very much got said.

For the Rigmaroles, they had yet to ever encounter a creature like the one now approaching the outer gate of the town.

The Trump strolled down the cobblestone pathway until he came to a small garden gate with an even smaller bronze plaque that was inscribed "Rigmarole Town".

Brandishing the shovel, the creature with the head of a peach reared back to strike the gate when a voice shouted out.

"Wait!!! What are you doing?!" shouted the small, stout man in the waistcoat and pantaloons. "You can't just do that!"

The Trump grew anxious at being told no and furrowed his brow at the strangely-dressed stranger. The hair tensed up and laid perfectly still, watching for something…

The peach started to speak when the man introduced himself as Benson Bailywick, the Keeper of the Gate.

For a full ten minutes, Benson Bailywick extolled the virtues of a solid gate and its purpose related to the short picket fence that surrounded Rigmarole Town.

"Why a picket fence and not a wall?" The Trump asked. "Seems to me a wall would keep out people much better than a fence."

Benson Bailywick laughed for a moment, then gave another long-winded speech; this one about lands and cultures and the freedom to move about.

"Walls don't work. They only inhibit the view and restrain the spirit," the Keeper of the Gate explained. "Besides, we welcome all newcomers, just so long as they think like us… and are able to tell us so."

Just then, a familiar figure appeared strolling down the cobblestone path.

"Greetings, kind sir!" the Tin Woodman exclaimed.

"And just who… or what are you?!" The Trump replied.

"Please allow me to introduce myself. I am Emperor Nicholas III of the House of Chopper. I have come from the Winkie Country to meet you and see who you may be," the Tin Woodman replied.

"An Emperor, you say? That must be good… and you come to see me?" The Trump asked.

Before the Tin Woodman could reply, The Trump launched his own verbal routine, which had served him well so far in the Land of Oz.

He heaped loads of praise upon the Tin Woodman, complimenting him about this and that... and even some of the other. He spoke of knuckleheads and witch hunts, climate change and impeachment, none of which had any meaning to the Tin Woodman... or Benson Bailywick.

"Seeing that you are royalty," The Trump observed, "I thought you might make a great Acting Attorney General in my administration."

Emperor Nicholas III of the House of Chopper felt thoroughly overwhelmed by the onslaught of The Trump's praises and embellishments and swooned at the offer.

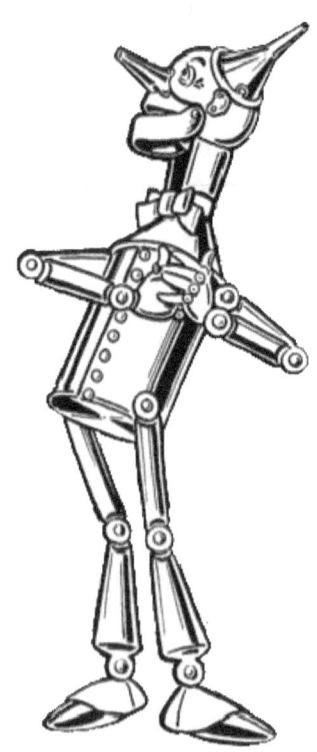

The Tin Woodman hadn't noticed the hair puffing itself up and assuming a more relaxed position.

"Your first duty as Acting Attorney General is to carry my shovel!" The Trump demanded. He tossed the shovel at the Tin Woodman, who caught it deftly.

Emperor Nicholas III of the House of Chopper fondled the shovel lovingly. It was a new thing and both like and unlike his trusty axe.

"Check this shit out," the peach whispered to his new Acting Attorney General, who was taken aback by the new word.

"Hey you there! What's your name! Uuuuh, Benadryl, that's right!" The Trump shouted. "What was that thing you were talking about a minute ago?"

They watched and listened as Benson Bailywick launched into another topic regarding something or other… They weren't too sure what.

As the Keeper of the Gate droned on and on about that thing he had been talking about earlier, a crowd began to gather from Rigmarole Town.

Soon, they were cheering and replying with long-winded answers to even the simplest statement.

"See?" The Trump said as he poked the Tin Woodman in the chest. "These people won't stop talking. How can they appreciate my genius if I can't get a word in edgewise? Don' they realize that I know more than any of them ever will?"

"They're Rigmaroles. What did you expect?" the Tin Woodman replied. "Princess Ozma sends them here so that they won't bother anyone else with their long-windedness."

The Trump pursed his lips and seemed to have a thought regarding something as the hair rippled slightly.

Just then, it appeared as if Benson Bailywick was coming to his long-winded conclusion.

"This isn't philogrobilizing but, being callipygian, shivviness is common. So, I'm fudgeling and perendinating about kakistocracies, and arguing with ultracrepidanian grumbletonians who twattle about snollygosters. There - that wasn't so hard then?" Benson Bailywick suggested.

Everyone in attendance looked over at The Trump, eager to gauge its reaction to Benson Bailywick's diatribe.

Another ripple subtly passed through the hair as it reshuffled its position and resumed its passive stance.

The Trump seemed pleased by the unwavering attention now paid to his presence and pressed his chest outward.

"MAKE OZ GREAT AGAIN!!!" he shouted, then turned and tapped the Tin Woodman on the chest. "Let's blow this joint."

The Trump and his new Acting Attorney General beat a hasty retreat as the Rigmaroles shouted and chanted "Make Oz great again," over and over again.

"Always leave'em wanting more," The Trump confided to the Tin Woodman, who was still in shell-shock from before, as they quickly strolled up to the crossroads and took a definite right towards the west and onward.

Chapter 16
The Unquenchable Rust

It was near sundown when The Trump and his Acting Attorney General approached a signpost that read:

"Who are these losers?" The Trump asked.

"These are the Flutterbudgets, though I wouldn't call them 'losers'," the Tin Woodman replied. "They're more like folks with really vivid imaginations."

"Whad'ya mean?" asked The Trump.

"They worry over the least little thing like it's the end of the world," the Acting Attorney General explained. "And their fears know no boundaries."

The Trump perked up a bit and the Tin Woodman noticed the hair on top of the large peach for the first time.

It seemed to pulsate slightly at the thought of the Flutterbudgets.

"Sounds like my kinda folks! You know… Dumbasses!!!" The Trump declared.

The Tin Woodman scratched his head, puzzled by yet another new word.

The Trump headed down the pathway that led south from the road of red brick, followed by his Acting Attorney General.

In a matter of minutes, the two of them found themselves in the town square of Flutterbudget Center and at the mercy of the locals.

"Pardon me sir," a man in yellow said as he passed by. "I have to get indoors before I get struck by lightning!"

The Trump looked up at the clear skies above, now ablaze with the colors of evening twilight as the Great Sun of Oz had set in the east moments before.

"But there's not a cloud in the skies!" The Trump shouted to the retreating man.

"No matter!" he shouted back. "If the clouds do appear, I'll surely be struck by lightning!"

The man in yellow continued on into the nearby set of houses.

"Watch out for my cat, sir!" exclaimed the lady in the blue bonnet, who gestured wildly at the approaching feline. "If you're not careful, you'll cause him to spill my drink!"

The Trump watched as the cat, who was walking upright and carrying a tray with a glass of wine, reacting to the wild gesturing, proceeded to stumble and spill the tray and its contents.

The Trump laughed loudly as the lady in the blue bonnet complained nearly as loud.

"If you hadn't come along, I'd have my drink by now!" she declared. "And now, I'll never be able to set foot in Emerald City again!"

"When was the last time you were in Emerald City?" the Acting Attorney General politely asked.

"Never!" came the response as the lady in blue and her cat strolled off into another area of houses along the town square.

The Tin Woodman looked at The Trump and shrugged his shoulders.

"See what I mean?" the Tin Woodman asked. "The littlest thing becomes the end of the world to these people. That's why they're brought here to live."

"Really?" The Trump replied. The hair once more perked up at the conversation.

"Yes. The Flutterbudgets and the Rigmaroles live in these two defensive settlements in order to defend Oz from their… peculiarities," the Tin Woodman explained.

The hair began waving as if driven by a gentle breeze and the Tin Woodman found himself mesmerized by its gentle waving.

The Trump seized upon the moment and hoisted himself, with great difficulty, up onto the low red brick wall that surrounded the town fountain.

"My friends!" he shouted, "My friends!! My friends!!!"

By now, the entire population of Flutterbudget Center, which numbered about a three dozen or so, were gathered together in front of the town fountain, equally mesmerized by the creature with the head of a peach.

"I've got some terrific news that'll solve all your problems, and I know you have many! Believe me when I say that the Unquenchable Rust is coming your way and we've gotta be doing something that is beautiful and perfect." The Trump declared.

The Tin Woodman watched in awe as The Trump preached about this and that… and even some of the other.

"If I hadn't come along, why my Acting Attorney General here would've melted away when struck by the Unquenchable Rust!" The Trump exclaimed, gesturing all the while.

"But I'm made of tin, which doesn't ru..." the Tin Woodman tried to explain.

"Believe me, he's wrong!" The Trump interrupted loudly while pointing at the Tin Woodman. "Anything else is fake news and a witch hunt!!"

At the mere mention of a witch, the locals went quite berserk with fear and hyperbole. The Trump watched gleefully as the Flutterbudgets argued among themselves about the Unquenchable Rust and witch hunts, in between bouts of chanting "The Trump! The Trump! The Trump!"

The hair was now fully engaged in the proceedings and seemed almost to be conducting the Flutterbudgets like an orchestra.

The Tin Woodman, who was beyond mesmerized by the actions of the hair and the words of The Trump found himself perplexed and confused.

"This Unquenchable Rust sounds horrible," he thought to himself. *"My tin body can't rust, but if The Trump says so, it must be true."*

As The Trump repeated his claims about the Unquenchable Rust, the Tin Woodman found himself chanting "The Trump!" over and over again in unison with the crowd.

The Trump turned around and smiled back at his Acting Attorney General, pleased that he had converted yet another "fool" to his cause.

Chapter 17
Hamburders & Cofefe

It was suggested by several of the Flutterbudgets that the gathering should make its way indoors in case of Oz quakes, tornadoes or some other calamity.

In time, The Trump and his admiring crowd of Flutterbudgets found themselves in the town hall, chanting, shouting and generally worrying about every little thing The Trump warned them about.

In particular, the Unquenchable Rust seemed to worry them the most and The Trump played upon their fears with a constant stream of warnings.

"If we do nothing, everything you believe in will be consumed by the Unquenchable Rust and you will all be destroyed!!! We must Make Oz Great Again!!!" he shouted at the cheering throngs. The Tin Woodman was now fully immersed in the fear mongering and was The Trump's loudest and most ardent supporter.

By now, the hair had calmed down and resumed its passive posture, assured that the crowds were now fully converted and willing to believe virtually anything.

The chanting, fear mongering and overwhelming adulation of the Flutterbudgets went on for hours as the crowds slowly diminished.

By midnight, only a few citizens of Flutterbudget Center remained as the rest retired to their homes to wallow in the fears and worries that The Trump had stoked in them.

The Trump looked over the remaining few Flutterbudgets and recognized the lady in the blue bonnet who had complained about her cat earlier that evening.

"You there!" he shouted, pointing at her."What's your name?"

"Minerva Menses, sir," she said timidly.

"I can see that you're a person of quality and I'm gonna give you a great honor," The Trump declared proudly. "You get to have me stay in your home tonight. I haven't slept in a real bed since I got here and I need a couple of hours of sleep and some decent food!"

Minerva Menses was beside herself with joy. She was stunned that she was permitted the honor of having The Trump stay at her home for the night. All memory of her earlier encounter had faded away with the drumbeat of "The Trump" pounding loudly in her head.

"Make sure you have some hamburders for me to eat!" he demanded as they made their way across the town square towards her home. "And don't forget the cofefe either!"

Minerva wasn't sure what hamburders or cofefe were, so her fears and concerns only grew as they entered her small home.

Chapter 18
Hats

The Scarecrow bid his guests farewell at the entrance of his Corn Mansion and watched as they headed towards Emerald City.

A Messenger Crow soon lighted upon his shoulder and whispered in The Scarecrow's ear, causing him to pace about and think about things.

After a few minutes, The Scarecrow was on his way eastward to Emerald City and the Palace of Princess Ozma. Over a hundred years of walking it, The Scarecrow was confident he could make Her Majesty's Place by sunrise the following day. He looked up to note the position of the Great Sun and surmised it must be about 8 in the morning.

The Scarecrow, having mastered the art of walking long ago, was making good time. The locals along the way had witnessed this march many times before and could tell when it was a happy walk or a serious walk. By all accounts it was a serious walk and the locals, be they Winkies or citizens of Emerald City Country, knew better than to delay The Scarecrow.

By sunrise of the next morning, The Scarecrow was making his way along the streets of Emerald City, greeting the citizens as he walked towards the Grand Palace that towered over the city square.

Princess Ozma came running down the steps and gave The Scarecrow the warm embrace of a fellow ruler.

"Thank you for coming so quickly," Princess Ozma said softly. "It is an odd thing, requiring your unique abilities, that brings you to Our Court, My dear friend."

The two retired to the inner palace Throne Room for their usual game of checkers.

"And how, Your Majesty, may I be of service to You now?" The Scarecrow asked politely. He knew full well that these games of checkers were Princess Ozma's way of sharing knowledge and seeking advice.

Princess Ozma was both kind and gentle as the Ruler of Oz. She made it a point to respect and value the opinion of every one of Her subjects, including The Scarecrow.

She spent the next dozen games or so explaining to The Scarecrow all the "goings-on, as Princess Dorothy would say."

"Can we look at it now?" The Scarecrow asked.

"Of course," She replied. "It's always best to acquire as much information as possible if one is to make a responsible decision."

The Scarecrow nodded in agreement with Her Majesty. He always marveled at Her wisdom and patience, and especially the information She had just spoken to him.

Soon, the Magic Picture was showing them The Trump and the Tin Woodman, apparently having a discussion in front of a small house in Flutterbudget Center. Princess Ozma recognized it as the home of Minerva Menses, where She had observed The Trump and the Tin Woodman arrive the night before.

By now, Glinda had joined in the watching of The Trump. She was pleased to see that the Tin Woodman was standing his ground against the very rude creature with the head of a giant peach.

"Is Princess Dorothy joining us today?" Glinda inquired. She looked about in search of Princess Ozma's dearest and closest friend, but did not see her... or Toto too.

"She is staying with Aunt Em and Uncle Henry in their cottage just north of Emerald City," Princess Ozma replied. "She was quite distraught witnessing that thing assault you like it did. I imagine the comfort of family right now is just what she needs."

"What is The Trump doing with that shovel?" The Scarecrow said, pointing at the Magic Picture as The Trump slammed the shovel down into the ground before it.

Suddenly, a gush of red something or another came forth from the hole in the ground made by the shovel. Everyone looked at it with much puzzlement when the old former Wizard of Oz showed up behind them and answered their questions.

"Those are hats, I do believe..."

Chapter 19
The Procession of
The Trump

The Trump reached out his hand and demanded his shovel from the Tin Woodman.

"What kind of an Acting Attorney General are you anyways?!" The Trump shouted.

"I haven't a clue what you're referring to?" Emperor Nicholas III of the House of Chopper inquired as he handed the shovel to the creature with the head of a giant peach.

"You wouldn't leave… Dammit!! I could'a nailed that broad if it weren't for you!" The Trump exclaimed. He pointed back at the door they had just came from.

"Why would you want to nail her? Wouldn't that injure her greatly? What did she ever do to you?" the Tin Woodman asked. He had spent the night standing guard inside at the doorway of Minerva Menses' home, much to the dismay of The Trump. "Besides, it's a matter of honor to stand guard against villains, be they my subjects or Ozma's, or Glinda's," the Tin Woodman explained. He found himself staring at The Trump's hair, which was now very agitated and pointing at him menacingly.

"Just remember this…" The Trump whispered as he leaned into the Tin Woodman.

Just then, the hair stretched outward and slapped Emperor Nicholas III of the House of Chopper upside the head, which resulted in a dull thud sound.

"Never get between a dog and his bone!!!" The Trump shouted. He swung hard and planted the shovel deep into the soil below.

The Emperor of the Winkies was more stunned than injured and watched wordlessly as a fountain of something red emerged from the hole left by the shovel.

He gazed in amazement as The Trump reached down and plucked something red from the stream of red and put it on his head.

In plain Ozian letters on the front, it read:

MOGA

The hair tried to peek out from beneath, but The Trump tucked it in and paraded around the gathering crowd.

"Make Oz Great Again!!!" he shouted. Within seconds, the entire square was filled with Flutterbudgets, all shouting "Make Oz Great Again" over and over.

The Trump scooped up armfuls of hats and flung them out to the adoring crowds. In turn, everyone there donned a hat and turned the town square into a sea of red.

"We're going to Emerald City to Make Oz Great Again!!!" The Trump announced to the adoring crowds. "Now someone get me a limo! I'm tired of walking!!!"

It took the Flutterbudgets a few moments to decipher what The Trump wanted, which was a wagon with a comfortable seat. Despite being a defensive settlement, the Flutterbudgets did engage in commerce on a rare occasion, and so there were a wagon or two to pick from.

And thus The Trump and his Acting Attorney General set out for the Emerald City, pulled along by various Flutterbudgets, who often fought to be allowed to pull The Trump.

"It is a beautiful thing you do," The Trump would say to each Flutterbudget as they took their turn pulling The Trump in the procession.

Minerva Menses was nowhere to be seen, having barricaded herself up in her bedroom during the night.

When she awoke the next morning, she found herself alone in the town and at peace with herself. With no one left to feed her fears, they left her… one by one, until she was whole once more.

Minerva Menses then packed her things and left for places unknown; where it is rumored she found happiness and joy… and even Love.

Chapter 20
Dorothy & Toto

The little farm girl from Kansas found herself back in her Royal Quarters within the Royal Palace of Princess Ozma, pondering her choices and actions; her precious dog Toto, by her side.

Her stay with Aunt Em and Uncle Henry had been very pleasant and helpful, given how upset she had been when she arrived.

"I tell you Toto, we'll deal with this bully the way Aunt Em said to," Dorothy said confidently.

Toto, being a dog of few words, just panted and stared at her. He was certain of Dorothy's intent and as usual, remained silent and vigilant.

By mid-morning, Dorothy had joined Princess Ozma and Glinda in the main Throne Room.

She was pleased when The Scarecrow showed up and embraced him warmly.

"Oh Scarecrow!" Dorothy exclaimed. "It was an awful thing that creature did to Glinda!"

"I know. Glinda explained it to me earlier and I'm still angry about it," The Scarecrow said softly. He was embarrassed at being angry, since all of Oz knew him to be a happy creature whenever possible. This time however, it was not possible.

"Aunt Em set me straight on what that thing is. She called it a bully, and she's right…. And there's only one way to deal with a bully," Dorothy replied.

The Scarecrow decided not to press Dorothy on what to do with a bully, having recalled an old lesson that taught *Ignorance Is Bliss*.

Princess Ozma cleared Her throat and a hush filled the Throne Room.

"Aunt Em is a wise woman indeed, though I must admit that Uncle Henry gave me a wonderful idea to deal with this Trump creature," said Princess Ozma.

Dorothy decided not to press Princess Ozma on what Uncle Henry had suggested, having recalled the same old lesson that taught *Ignorance Is Bliss*.

Chapter 21
Near Miss

By the time the Procession of The Trump had landed on the Road of Red Brick, a large gathering of Rigmaroles had appeared from the east. They seemed hell-bent on joining the procession, though it took over an hour before the countless speeches ended and The Trump commanded that they move on.

Within the hour, the vegetation had changed from predominantly red to predominantly yellow.

"We're in my realm now," the Tin Woodman explained. "This is Winkie Country, of which I am Emperor Nicholas III of the House of Chopper."

"Emperor, you say?" replied The Trump.

"Yes. When the Wizard gave me a heart, I found Love and compassion once more and was proclaimed Emperor of the Winkies," the Tin Woodman declared as he patted his chest.

The Trump thought to ask a question when a crossroad came into view and he became distracted.

The crowd came to a sudden halt as the Procession of The Trump did the same. A murmur ran through the Rigmaroles and Flutterbudgets as The Trump stood up in the wagon and surveyed the scene.

In the center of the crossroad, where all four red brick roads met, was a signpost which pointed northeast for Emerald City and southwest for the Truth Pond.

"What's that mean? Truth pond? Seriously???" The Trump demanded.

"It's a pond located near the Deadly Desert that can remedy unwanted enchantments, but at a cost," the Emperor of the Winkies explained.

"What cost?" The Trump inquired. The hair slicked back and flattened out.

"A dip in the waters of the Truth Pond will compel one to speak only the Truth forevermore," the Emperor said.

At once, The Trump looked around and saw a sea of red MOGA hats. Even the Rigmaroles had managed to score hats from the Flutterbudgets, who had more than they would ever need, though they would argue that they'll never have enough for some reason or another.

The hair fluffed back up and resumed its normal odd look, which now reminded the Tin Woodman of Dorothy's dear friend from Kansas, Billina the Hen.

The Trump pointed towards Emerald City and a cheer arose from the admiring crowds.

"It's time to Lock Her Up!" The Trump shouted across the MOGA sea.

The crowd immediately erupted into chants of "Lock Her Up, Lock Her Up, Lock Her Up!"

He sat down next to his Acting Attorney General as the Procession of The Trump continued onward towards the Emerald City.

"Whew!" The Trump said as he retrieved a handkerchief from his coat pocket and wiped his brow. "That was a near miss, wasn't it?"

Chapter 22
Memories Of The Nome King

Dorothy watched the Magic Picture as the Procession of The Trump made its way towards the Emerald City, passing through the Winkie Country and stopping to give speeches and such.

She had decided to apply another lesson of Aunt Em and get as much information as possible before something happened. Princess Ozma was more than happy to oblige as She found Aunt Em to be a wise woman, as was Uncle Henry a wise man.

As Dorothy watched the speech of the creature with a giant peach for a head, a silly thought crossed her mind and she began to giggle. Mind you, it was a soft giggle, but a giggle nonetheless.

Princess Ozma, who was sitting on Her throne noticed and caught Her ear to Her dearest friend in Oz, Dorothy Gale of Kansas.

"What gives you the giggles, My dear?" Princess Ozma inquired.

"Just a silly memory," Dorothy replied. "That creature's hair reminded me of the old Nome King… You know the one? Old Roquat of the Rocks."

Princess Ozma knew a good joke when She heard one and returned Dorothy's giggle. Then a thought crossed Her mind and the wisdom of Love and Immortality gave Her a thought to think about.

Chapter 23
Somnium

The Great Trump rose steadily in the west as the Land of Oz awoke, refreshed and ready for another day; although what kind of a day it would become was as much a mystery to one as to all.

Of course, everyone in Oz had known it as the Great Sun and would welcome it with open arms and open eyes as the people of Oz loved the Great Sun.

Everyone knew it as that until that day when The Trump had accomplished the impossible.

He had come down from the Mountain of the Hammerheads, where he declared himself "free of the Knuckle-Heads" and began his journey towards the Emerald City.

In time, The Trump had marched on the Emerald City, gained the Power of Oz and bombastically declared himself Emperor of Oz.

It was then that the people of Oz demanded that the Great Sun be renamed The Great Trump as a tribute to their new glorious leader.

Chapter 24
The Shovel

The Trump awoke with a start as the Procession of The Trump crossed into Emerald City Country, where everything was predominantly green.

"Good morning," the Tin Woodman said. "You didn't sleep long."

The Trump shook his head and the hair fluffed up and rearranged itself into its usual wave.

"I've just had the most wonderful dream. It was a beautiful thing," The Trump said. He looked around at the surrounding countryside.

"Where are we?" he asked. "Everything's green now."

"Of course. We've entered the Emerald City Country. It would seem your supporters have been making good time pulling this wagon," the Tin Woodman explained. "If you look to the eastern horizon where that green glow is, you can just make out the Emerald City.

The Trump seemed unimpressed by the distant sight of glowing green buildings. He scanned the crowd that was accompanying him and saw that the MOGA Sea had nearly doubled in size since before his short nap earlier.

Just then, the Procession of The Trump came ambling up to a wide river and a stone-arched bridge crossing it. Once a new set of people had volunteered to pull the wagon and were hitched up, the Procession of The Trump crossed over it and headed towards the Emerald City.

"That was the Winkie River we just crossed," the Tin Woodman informed The Trump. "We should make the Emerald City by mid-day."

The Trump seemed pleased as he continued to shout out compliments to the crowd. Occasionally, shouts of "Lock Her Up! Lock Her Up!" would echo across the Emerald City Country as The Trump whipped the crowd up into a frenzy.

About half an hour after crossing the Winkie River, the Procession of The Trump came upon a large lake and The Trump suddenly became very agitated.

"I thought you said the Truth Pond was the other way!" he demanded of his Acting Attorney General. The hair once more slicked back and laid flat.

The Tin Woodman chuckled softly. "Goodness gracious. That's not the Truth Pond. That's Lake Quad, the largest lake in Oz," he said.

The hair relaxed a bit and The Trump seemed to calm down as well as they left Lake Quad behind them.

As the Emerald City grew closer, The Trump noticed that his Acting Attorney General was fondling the shovel once more.

"What's so important about this shovel that you have me carrying it for you?" the Emperor of the Winkies inquired.

The Trump chuckled as the wagon rattled and bumped along the wide cobblestone road leading northeast towards the green glow.

"Why, that shovel is how I got to this place... wherever this place is," The Trump informed his Acting Attorney General, who appeared puzzled by the response.

"It happened a few days ago, when I was talking to Rudy about digging up dirt on Joe Biden. He told me that he had all sorts of dirt on him and he showed me this shovel that he said he had used to dig it all up with," The Trump explained. "When I saw that shovel, I knew that it was exactly what I needed for another job that needed done. So I borrowed it from him."

"What kind of job?" the Acting Attorney General asked.

"Well, I told Rudy to get all my tax records together and I was going to bury them so no one would ever find them!" he exclaimed.

The Tin Woodman had no idea who Rudy was, let alone Joe Biden and he had absolutely no clue what tax records were. In fact, he had given up trying to understand most of what The Trump would say, as most of it seemed to be pure nonsense to him.

"So, I started looking around for a place to bury those dammed things when I ran across a small closet behind the bowling alley in the basement of the White House. It was perfect, so I took the shovel and I had Melania carry the box of records down there," The Trump continued on. "It took me an hour to pry up a part of the floor until I reached dirt. Then when I stuck the shovel into the dirt, the floor gave way and I fell into a long tunnel. All I could hear was that dumb bitch laughing at me as I fell down into the darkness. Then I ended up in a cave where something hairy attacked me in the darkness. After that, I came out of that dammed cave and…"

The Tin Woodman watched as The Trump told his tale of how he had arrived in Oz. He spoke about "descending an escalator", which really confused Emperor Nicholas III of the House of Chopper. It reminded him that those from the Great Outside came to Oz in odd and dangerous ways.

His dearest friend Dorothy had come to Oz by tornado the first time,

and by way of an earthquake another time.

She had even been thrown overboard with her hen,
Billina during an ocean voyage with Uncle Henry to
Australia and wound up in Oz.

The Emperor of the Winkies listened as The Trump bragged about Knuckleheads and China and some "wicked bitch".

The Acting Attorney General tried to get a word in whenever possible, but The Trump wouldn't stop talking.

Before long, he was ranting about something called NOAA and impeachment and other such nonsense the Tin Woodman didn't understand.

The crowd of Flutterbudgets, Rigmaroles and other locals from the surrounding countryside, as well as those pulling the wagon, listened intently and cheered at the slightest prompting by their new glorious leader, The Trump as the Procession of The Trump approached the Emerald City.

Chapter 25
Dorothy & Billina

After a few hours of watching the Magic Picture, Dorothy retired to her chambers to change into comfortable shoes. She then went out for a walk in search of her friend from Kansas who was neither a dog 'nor a cat.

She soon found herself outside the gardens behind the Royal Palace of Oz, where Billina the Hen; Queen and Governor of all the chickens in Oz lived.

"Dorothy, have you seen your grandmother?" Dorothy asked a nearby chicken.

"No Dorothy, I haven't. Let me ask my sister, Dorothy," the nearby chicken replied.

"Dorothy!!!" the nearby chicken shouted.

"Here, Dorothy!" came the reply from another chicken nearby.

"Have you seen Grandma Billina?" the nearby chicken asked her sister, Dorothy.

Dorothy Gale rolled her eyes and chuckled to herself. She watched as the question resounded from sister to sister and daughter to granddaughter. This went on for over an hour by the time everyone had been asked and it was determined that Billina was not home.

It seems that in the slow progress of Time in Oz, Billina had managed to produce a fairly large family.

By her count, Billina was fairly certain she had well over a hundred hens, all of whom were named after her dearest friend, Dorothy Gale. They in turn had produced over a thousand hens themselves, as well as a number of what Billina described as "horrid roosters".

Billina had herself produced several "horrid roosters" herself, which she had then named Daniel. She only kept two around as that was as many as she could stand, along with several dozen hen daughters and granddaughters, whom she loved dearly. The rest, who were equally loved but were in the way, scattered across Oz to live their own lives, all of whom did and lived contented lives.

Dorothy soon made her escape from the gardens and found herself once more outside the walls of the Emerald City.

In time, she came upon Billina, who had been out searching for some new hay for a new nest.

"There you are, Billina!" Dorothy exclaimed as she scooped up the little yellow hen and embraced her warmly.

"I've been looking for you!" Dorothy said happily.

"Well, it seems you found me now, haven't you?" Billina replied.

Dorothy spent more than an hour explaining to Billina about The Trump and Glinda and China Country and the hair.

"Remember the Nome King and how he hated eggs?" Dorothy reminded the little yellow hen.

Billina remembered it well. She had found it odd that eggs were poisonous to Nomes

"Well, that creature's hair reminds me of the Nome King and I gotta hunch," said Dorothy.

"Count me in!" Billina exclaimed as she clucked merrily.

Dorothy and Billina headed back to the nearby Royal Palace.

Chapter 26
The Gates of the Emerald City

Princess Ozma found Dorothy walking about the grounds of the Royal Palace. The two of them talked for a while as Princess Ozma explained Her plan for dealing with the approaching menace.

The Royal Ruler of Oz was convinced that there was a peaceful way out of the situation, but Dorothy had other plans.

"That creature is a bully!" Dorothy exclaimed. "And the only way to deal with a bully is to confront them!"

Princess Ozma smiled and nodded Her head. She knew Dorothy well enough to know that the little farm girl from Kansas had something interesting planned for the creature with the head of a giant peach.

Dorothy soon made her way back to her quarters within the palace as Princess Ozma headed towards the large emerald-encrusted gates that served as the main entrance into Emerald City.

In time, the Royal Ruler of Oz had made Her way past the large gates and stood ready to greet the new visitor from the Great Outside.

Chapter 27
Theresa May

The MOGA Sea seemed nearly as large as Lake Quad as it approached the Gates of the Emerald City.

At the head of the large chanting masses was a wagon bearing The Trump and his Acting Attorney General, the Tin Woodman.

"Who's the broad with the crown?!" the creature with the head of a giant peach exclaimed.

"Why, that's Princess Ozma, Royal Ruler of Oz. She's here to greet us, as is Her custom," the Tin Woodman replied.

"Pffttt! Bullshit!" The Trump countered. "She's looks a little young for me anyways. Besides, she ain't got blonde hair... like Ivanka." He leered at his Acting Attorney General, who didn't appear to understand. "That's more Jeffrey's thing anyways."

The Tin Woodman thought to ask who Jeffrey was, but thought better of it.

Just then, the chanting masses and the wagon came to an abrupt halt.

"Greetings... and welcome to Emerald City and the Land of Oz. I am Ozma, Ruler of Oz, and I welcome you to My Kingdom," the Royal Ruler of Oz proclaimed.

Her voice ran through the MOGA Sea and connected with every citizen of Oz present.

As a Half-Fairy Immortal and the child of King Pastoria, a mortal king of Oz and Queen Lurline, Goddess Over All and the First Immortal; Princess Ozma commanded the compassion and nobility of wisdom, wit and wonder that Time had permitted Her.

The effect was noticeable to all in attendance. Be they Flutterbudgets, Rigmaroles or the other locals from the surrounding countryside, as well as those pulling the wagon; they were all citizens of Oz and each one uniquely attuned to the Daughter of Lurline and Pastoria.

The Hair on The Trump stood up tall and looked about, seeking a kindred spirit… and finding none.

The Tin Woodman, who was also smitten by Princess Ozma's greeting, watched as The Trump launched into his usual routine of insults, mis-truths and diversions as he whipped the crowds up into a frenzy.

In a matter of minutes, the MOGA Sea was once more a seething, rabid mass of discontent against the Royal Ruler of Oz.

The Trump turned towards Princess Ozma, who had been patiently awaiting his reply to Her greeting.

"Hey toots, is your man around here somewhere?" it asked.

Princess Ozma seemed puzzled as She looked around.

"I beg your pardon?" She asked.

"Your man… You know, the one who actually runs this place," The Trump replied.

Princess Ozma furrowed Her brow and paused to consider the creature now in front of Her.

"No man has ruled Oz since the days of King Pastoria, who happens to be–"the Tin Woodman tried to explain when The Trump interrupted him.

"Bullshit!!!" it exclaimed. "Any broad running a country is a loser! Just look at that Merkel broad. Stupid bitch thinks she knows it all. I know more than she'll ever know. Hell, she thought Hitler was wrong."

Princess Ozma narrowed Her gaze towards The Hair on top of the ranting, raving peach. It gazed back and shifted position without The Trump missing a beat.

"What was that cunt's name that ran England? You know, the one that ain't the queen?" The Trump asked his Acting Attorney General. "Sounded like a month or some shit like that."

The Tin Woodman shrugged his shoulders. He had no clue what the creature with a giant peach for a head was spouting about now. In fact, he hadn't understood a word The Trump uttered since meeting him at Flutterbudget Center.

Princess Ozma shifted Her attention to the crowd surrounding the wagon and noticed a disturbing trend. Nearly every citizen of the MOGA Sea was livid with each utterance from The Trump. She watched as it shouted various nonsense and such, with the crowd reacting almost on cue.

The Hair had grown even bolder as it pulsated about and conducted the MOGA Sea like a fine orchestra.

Princess Ozma watched The Hair as it went about its business. She paused a moment and a memory from more than a century ago made itself known.

The Royal Ruler of Oz now understood the creature ranting and raving before Her. She returned Her gaze to the wagon and The Trump, now trying its best to exit the wagon without falling over. It failed miserably, much to its embarrassment and shame.

Chapter 28
The Queen of the Field Mice

The Trump struggled to get up as the Tin Woodman nimbly hopped over the low rail and onto the cobblestone of the Emerald City Country.

All around, the MOGA Sea struggled to deal with the sight of their glorious leader lying spread-eagle on the smooth stone.

The Acting Attorney General looked down at his glorious leader and all compassion seemed to fade away.

Finally, the Tin Woodman reached out a nickel-plated hand and helped The Trump to its feet. He watched as the peach launched into another tirade that seemed to last forever.

"He pushed me! You saw it?!" The Trump shouted at his Acting Attorney General for all to hear. "Lock him up, lock him up!!!"

For several minutes, the MOGA Sea chanted the refrain until Princess Ozma gently and politely cleared Her throat and all ceased talking.

The silence of the MOGA Sea was deafening, both to the peach and the hair. Neither could utter a sound or make a move. Only the rustle of sawgrass on the edge of the cobblestone shook everyone to their senses.

Princess Ozma looked down and smiled at the diminutive rodent with the shining gold crown.

"Your Majesty, how exquisite it is to see you this fine day," the Royal Ruler said to the Queen of the Field Mice.

Before the Royal Rodent could answer, The Trump managed to let loose a blood-curdling scream that rattled the teeth of everyone present, including both Queens.

"Goodness gracious!" the Queen of the Field Mice exclaimed. "Whatever are those creatures?"

The Trump backed away slowly; grabbing anyone it could to shield it from "that thing!"

The Hair slicked itself back and laid low

"You! Acting Attorney General! Git rid of that vile thing! Kill it!!!" The Trump screamed at Emperor Nicholas III of the House of Chopper. "Kill that fucking thing now!!!"

117

Princess Ozma gasped audibly. It had been a long time, even by Her standards, since She had witnessed such a display of vile, cruel anger in its purest form.

With silence falling upon everyone present, the only sound came from The Trump, who felt a need to whimper and hide behind his Acting Attorney General.

The Tin Woodman looked back at The Trump and saw in its face the sum of all that was wrong at that moment. He reached down and scooped up the diminutive rodent in his hand.

"Have no fear, Your Majesty. I will permit no harm to befall you," Emperor Nicholas III of the House of Chopper assured the Queen.

The Trump became livid with his Acting Attorney General and began a long tirade against him.

The MOGA Sea joined in with every insult, chanting loudly and with great enthusiasm as The Trump berated and degraded his Acting Attorney General.

The Tin Woodman stood there, with the Queen of the Field Mice in hand as The Trump went on for what seemed like hours, though in truth, it was merely a matter of minutes. They both looked at each other in disbelief as the creature with the head of a giant peach droned on and on about betrayal, liars, and various other things neither the Tin Woodman nor the Queen of the Field Mice understood.

"What is it going on about?" the Royal Rodent inquired.

"I have no clue," the Tin Woodman replied. "In fact, since I've met it, I haven't understood a single thing it talks about."

Before the Queen of the Field Mice could reply, a familiar and beloved creature of Oz came running up to the feet of Princess Ozma.

Chapter 29
Toto

By now, The Trump had ceased its tirade against the Acting Attorney General and was drinking some water from a large mug handed to it by one of the members of the MOGA Sea.

As it slowly drank, several of the wagon crew began laughing at how The Trump had to use two hands to lift the mug to its lips.

In time, they began to realize that their new hero may not be what they had hoped for and several of them abandoned their position at the front of the wagon.

Within moments, several Flutterbudgets from the MOGA Sea had taken their place and were joking about the departing folks, all of whom were Rigmaroles.

Princess Ozma watched as The Hair turned about on the peach and watched the Rigmaroles as they headed back south towards their home village.

Just then, The Trump turned about and shouted at the departing group.

"Losers!!! Liars!!! All of you!!! You're not worthy of being a part of my entourage. You're just scum!!!" it shouted with glee as the MOGA Sea joined in the harangue.

Princess Ozma was now convinced who was actually in charge of the chanting crowd before Her.

As the group of Rigmaroles slowly faded from view, Toto took notice of the creature with the head of a giant peach. A low, slow growl began to emerge from the little black dog with long silky hair.

"Goodness gracious Toto. What's wrong?" Princess Ozma asked the little dog, whose growling was growing stronger and more pronounced.

"That creature is Evil!" Toto exclaimed. "And the thing below it too!"

The Trump turned towards Toto and suddenly kicked the little dog, sending it rolling across the smooth stone with a yelp.

"Kill that dog! Do it now!!!" The Trump demanded of his Acting Attorney General. "When I'm Emperor, no dogs will be allowed here!!!"

The MOGA Sea grew silent once more, stunned at their leader's eagerness to kill an innocent mouse and a beloved dog. Even the Flutterbudgets balked at the idea of killing any creature, let alone Toto, who they all knew and loved.

Princess Ozma, horrified by The Trump's violence against Toto, brandished her Royal Scepter and approached the creature with the head of a giant peach.

"Enough of that nonsense!" Princess Ozma exclaimed. A hint of anger was in Her voice and everyone there knew it.

She then knelt down to comfort the small dog, who was shaking his head and nursing several sore ribs.

Chapter 30
You're Fired!

The Tin Woodman was speechless during the exchange between Toto, The Trump and Princess Ozma. His mind raced with thoughts that conflicted with what his heart believed. He leaned down and gently set the Queen of the Field Mice down upon the smooth stone.

"Thank you," said the Royal Rodent.

She looked up into his eyes and smiled.

"You might want to take a closer look at those creatures... before you become one of them," she exclaimed before scurrying off into the nearby sawgrass.

Emperor Nicholas III of the House of Chopper looked carefully at The Trump, who suddenly seemed weak and pitiful. He began to realize that The Trump was not what it appeared to be. He saw in the creature a look of self-loathing, arrogance and self-importance, all of which came into direct conflict with what he knew to be right and proper.

The Hair rustled about atop the giant peach as The Trump began to approach Princess Ozma with an Evil glare in its eyes.

"Come on, babe! You know you want it. They always do. Hell, I can do anything I want! Every woman thinks I'm a god!!!" The Trump declared confidently as it approached the Princess with its arms outstretched.

Once more, Princess Ozma brandished Her Royal Scepter and poked The Trump harshly in the chest, causing a large shower of green sparks and sending the creature with the head of a giant peach staggering backwards.

Her anger was clear and focused as She watched The Hair shudder and slick itself back.

The MOGA Sea was once again speechless as their new hero struggled to speak.

"Did I understand you to say that you intend to become Emperor of Oz?" the Royal Ruler of Oz inquired.

"Why shouldn't I?" The Trump demanded. "After all, no broad can do a better job than me!"

"I wasn't talking to you!" Princess Ozma shouted at The Trump, who seemed perplexed by Her response. Everyone else was dumbstruck by Her Majesty's angry outburst.

The Tin Woodman, who had been silent throughout the whole episode, had finally had enough.

"That's it! I've had enough of you!" the Tin Woodman declared. He reached back into the satchel on his back and retrieved the shovel that he had once idolized.

"I've watched as you've treated everyone around you like dirt!" Emperor Nicholas III of the House of Chopper exclaimed. "Over and over, I've turned a blind eye to your narcissistic, misogynistic attitudes towards everyone around you, including me. I've watched as you tried to defile a woman, avoid the truth, outright lie, insult anyone who disagrees with you and plot to overthrow the most benevolent, wonderful ruler the Land of Oz has ever had!"

The Trump glared at his Acting Attorney General during his outburst. The Hair rolled over and seemed to whisper something into The Trump's ear.

"I'm done being your lackey... and I'm certainly done carrying this stupid shovel for you!" the Tin Woodman shouted as he threw the shovel hard into the ground, where it struck soft soil and stood upright.

By now, The Trump was clearly agitated by the Tin Woodman's outburst and Princess Ozma's refusal of its advances.

"What is your problem?!" The Trump demanded. "Don't you understand that without me, this place would be overrun by the Unquenchable Rust?! I'm the only hope this place has! You can't quit.... You're fired!!!"

126

The Tin Woodman turned to walk away, which seemed only to anger The Trump even more.

"Come on Toto. We're outta here! Let's find Dorothy," he said to the little black dog with long silky hair.

Chapter 31
The Letter

By now, a large crowd of citizens from the Emerald City had gathered behind Princess Ozma.

Like the MOGA Sea, they too were left speechless by Princess Ozma's outburst and the Tin Woodman's departure… and Toto too.

The Trump paraded about, fluffing itself and spouting random words in hope one would catch with the crowd. The crowd, for its part, was murmuring about this and that… and even some of the other.

Princess Ozma kept a keen eye on The Hair as She approached The Trump and addressed the pair.

"If you are set upon becoming Emperor of Oz, by what qualifications do you lay claim to the throne?" She inquired.

To all who heard Her Majesty speak, be they Flutterbudgets, Rigmaroles, Emerald City citizens or the assorted locals; each would agree that Her tone and authority was unquestionably noble, honest and true. It was Her most endearing quality and Her greatest asset.

The Trump fumbled about for a moment or two while The Hair lay flat and still. There was a stillness to the air that seemed almost magical, as one might expect in the Land of Oz.

Suddenly, The Trump kicked the upright shovel and knocked it over.

In the small trench left by the shovel appeared a small tan envelope peeking out from beneath the dirt.

The Trump reached down and grabbed it, holding it aloft and quickly began shouting.

"The letter! The letter!! The letter!!!" The Trump repeated, over and over as the MOGA Sea finally joined in.

The Trump thrust the letter towards the Royal Ruler of Oz, who backed away slightly and studied the creatures before Her.

Princess Ozma was uncertain if this parchment of sorts held any majikal properties, though She felt nothing emanating from it. Wisdom had taught Her long ago how to sense the difference between magic and majik.

"Read it out loud!" The Trump demanded.

The MOGA Sea now began a new chant that reverberated across the fields of green and the Emerald City.

"Read it! Read it! Read it!" the MOGA Sea chanted.

Princess Ozma listened to the echoes of the chant as they bounced to and fro across the bricks and stone of the Emerald City as the crowd came to a fever pitch.

Just then, She held aloft Her Royal Scepter and a hush fell upon most of the gathering while the Rigmaroles finished up their long-winded speeches. Then all was silent.

"As it is your letter, you should be the one to read it," Her Majesty said politely. She watched as The Trump stammered and struggled to get past the first few words.

The MOGA Sea began to murmur among themselves as the creature with the head of a giant peach looked about frantically.

The Hair also seemed to be searching about, though for what, Princess Ozma was uncertain.

Her Majesty looked about and observed keenly the reactions and emotions of the populace surrounding the wagon, The Trump and Herself.

A wave of pity and solace crossed Her mind as The Trump stopped talking and stood about, arms crossed tightly across its chest, clutching the letter tightly, a stern look upon its face.

"Reminds me of a pouting child," She thought to Herself as She reached towards the tightly-clutched letter.

Just then, the familiar blue-gloved hand of a former Ruler of Oz reached out and snatched it deftly from The Trump, who only grumbled a bit and pouted even more.

"Please allow me, Your Majesty," The Scarecrow said as he tried his best to un-wrinkle the letter.

Princess Ozma smiled warmly and nodded Her head towards Her predecessor.

The MOGA Sea became eerily quiet, as had The Trump. The Hair also remained motionless.

Holding the letter before him, the Scarecrow spoke in what everyone in attendance would later describe as a tone of knowledge and authority.

"A Memo On The Emperor's Health

By Dr. Vinnie Boom Batz

This letter is to certify that Donald Trump's enjoys continued robust good health, genius-plus level intellect, and physical perfection. As Oz's healthiest Emperor (and many people are saying) the healthiest human being in the world, Mr. Trump is a golden Adonis, a specimen of masculinity so perfect that in the annals of medical science we have been unable to find anyone who can rival him.

At 7 feet tall, Mr. Trump is our tallest Emperor, and at just 200 pounds, with body fat of 0 percent, he is undoubtedly the fittest Emperor, or indeed sovereign or head or state of any kind, in world history. While Mr. Trump is 73 years old, we assess his physical condition to be that of a 25-year-old elite athlete. His dedication to triathlons, daily weight training, and heavy cardio leaves his cadre of former Navy SEAL physical trainers shaking and exhausted, awed by his sheer endurance and power. As one told me during the preparation of this report, "Mr. Trump could easily complete BUDS/S tomorrow, then do the SFAS course simultaneously with the USAF Para-Rescue program, and then pass SERE with flying colors."

Mr. Trump has definitely, positively never, ever, ever had Gonorrhea, Herpes, Syphilis, Chlamydia, the French, Spanish, or English Pox, Crabs, Genital Lice, Crotch-Crickets, Bulgarian Junk-Rot, the Weeping Cobra, the Gift That Keeps On Giving, Studio 54 Stall Surprise, or the Bangkok Fire-Dick. Mr. Trump's noted fidelity to his wives should put to rest all of these scurrilous rumors. In fact, my laboratory research shows that contact with Mr. Trump's magnificent body kills all forms of STDs, and also cures Scrofula, Vertigo, Blindness, Sleep Apnea, and the Jimmy Leg.

Mr. Trump's daily routine is a model of health, not only for an Emperor but for any Ozian. Each day, Mr. Trump makes Oz great for eight hours, performs 10 hours of cardio, including strenuous golf-cart riding, hand cardio (Tweeting), and reporter haranguing. He then makes vigorous love to Mrs. Trump for five hours, sleeps one hour and repeats the process.

Mr. Trump's mental acuity transcends even the most aggressive projections for the far future of

Singularity-level Artificial Intelligences. His ability to consume volumes of complex intelligence materials in minutes leaves his staff in constant awe. Mr. Trump often demands his briefers present the original intel source material to him un-translated, since his ability to speak 124 languages is unrivaled.

When testing Mr. Trump's mental fitness, I discovered he had not only memorized the Code of Federal Regulations but could extemporaneously recite it in the form of a medieval French Chanson de Geste.

Mr. Trump's astounding power to understand and rectify complex, multivariate regulatory problems would be a bright display of his status as the most intelligent Emperor ever. Even knowing he was one of the most brilliant men in recorded history, his work on advanced string theory, quantum chromodynamics, and fusion containment is beyond my understanding as a mere medical man. Far from deserving just the Nobel Peace Prize, it is my humble opinion that Mr. Trump deserves Nobel Prizes in Literature, Economics, Chemistry, Physics, Medicine, and Making Oz Great Again.

His eyesight is so keen he can spot the panty line on an adult film actress from a half-mile. Mr. Trump's night vision is so acute he can read the text of a non-disclosure agreement printed in 4-point type in near-total darkness. The National Reconnaissance Office has asked the Emperor to allow them to make a model of his eyes to develop the next generation of surveillance satellite optics.

Mr. Trump's hearing is so acute that he can discern the faintest dog whistles and can detect any aspersions, insults, or questions regarding his character from miles away. In moments where Mr. Trump is seemingly unable to hear questions, his son-in-law Jared is happy to whisper in his ear, especially regarding his White House rivals.

Mr. Trump's genes display qualities heretofore unknown to science. They are, to use a term of scientific art, bigly superior. Careful analysis reveals that Mr. Trump's genetic sequences contain not only DNA and RNA, but also TNA, or Trump Nucleic Acids. TNA binds to gold leaf, golf greens, trophy wives, and self-regard. Although it is out of the purview of this report, I believe the only solution to the plague of Antifa Super-Soldiers threatening Oz is a clone army based on Mr. Trump's gloriously perfect and unique genetic makeup.

His hands are so very large that other Emperor's hands are like those of tiny, tiny dolls by comparison. Believe me. I measured them with extraordinary scientific rigor. My super-doctory scientific tests reveal that Mr. Trump's hands are also very, very strong. The Emperor can crush a titanium ingot like a marshmallow. He can palm bowling balls, and throw them over a mile without breaking a sweat. He has often carried weights heavier than any other Emperor, ever.

Mr. Trump's hair is thick, fast-growing, and retains its natural golden hue from his youth. His skin is that of a teenage farmgirl; smooth, taut, perfectly free of any wrinkles, moles, blemishes, wens, cystic formations, or signs of a lifetime of fast-food addiction, rough living, whoring, or long nights spent in the humid darkness of a low-rent Atlantic City casino.

Even for a man of Mr. Trump's astounding health, constitution, physical perfection, and genetic gifts, life is not without challenges.

Mr. Trump's body emits a thick musk of pure testosterone, causing men near him to become aggressive, and women to strip off their clothes and beg him to grab them by their reproductive organs. This powerful scent is a constant challenge to the Secret Service, as battalions of scantily-clad women wearing little but MOGA hats and thong panties throw themselves at the Emperor, forming human pyramids to scale security fences and showing up in attorney Michael Cohen's office demanding $130,000 payments.

Mr. Trump's manhood is, as you will be unsurprised to learn, is the largest of any Emperor, and in fact, larger than any mammalian penis outside that of the majestic blue whale. His genitals require a system of complex straps, buckles, pulleys, trusses, and velcro attachment points to contain them within his custom-fitted trousers.

As his very real physician (who many people say is the best medical expert from the best school ever, and totally not the pen name of an insecure man consumed by his petty vanities and insecurities) I certify the preceding to be really, really true.

Dr. Vinnie Boom Batz"

When the Scarecrow had finished his oratory, he looked up to see hundreds of open mouths and blank stares.

Only Princess Ozma had retained Her composure, though She was slightly disheveled by the entire reading.

"That was lovely…" Princess Ozma said matter-of-factly.

The Trump puffed up even more than before and The Hair swayed here and there in the gentle breeze.

Chapter 32
The Speech

Dorothy awoke from her nap, refreshed and ready for whatever lay ahead. She knew from her sources that Princess Ozma had allowed the odd creature and its companion hair into the heart of Emerald City for what Uncle Henry had described as "an election!"

"We's gonna vote the bum out!" Uncle Henry had shouted when Dorothy had asked "why?"

Now, the little girl from Kansas found herself sitting high above the crowds of Emerald City in Princess Ozma's Royal Box as her dear friend addressed the crowd.

"Citizen's of Oz, I present to you a supplicant for the position of Emperor. Judge rightly by its words,"

Princess Ozma announced. Her voice echoed gently before trailing off. "The audience is yours, Sir Trump."

The Trump, for its part, had been bragging about its early days in school to a group of locals when it turned its attention to the Ozians surrounding it.

"...Oh yes, I graduated, too, you know. Very intelligent. Good genes, very much smarts. You all have done well during these few years, and, well, I mean, let's say ... Not as good as I have, because, well, since, I have great and unmatched wisdom, you know, like, I know things, like, that even Nasa doesn't know.

Or maybe they do know it, I don't know, but they don't want you to know that they know. For instance: yuuuuge fact. Did you know that the Moon is a part of Mars? No? Much wisdom. Nasa says that the Moon is NOT a part of Mars...

FAKE NEWS!!! Nasa is the enemy of the people!! They keep the people stupid!! The Moon is the closest part of Mars!! Don't believe in Nasa. I had an uncle, very smart, and he told me, he really did, he said that, and I believe him, because he had much smarts, the Moon is in fact a part of Mars.

I promise I will put the most, really the very most, reliable and intelligent person I know as director of NASA, to make sure that the people who are hired by NASA, the people who will work there, those who will work on my Space Force, are all of the most smart people of the country. I have already discussed this with Donald junior, and, just like me, he knows, the truly does, very great, that he should be director of NASA, because he, just like me, has many smarts, and very good genes.

Do you want to buy a cap that says that? I hav'em made already. Very good. Very strong material. Excellent quality. All made in Oz!!! OZ FIRST!!!

It just says Made in China, because, too, obviously, well, it's clearly that, we have done that, to fool the IRS.

You have all paid very much to study, which is, uh, I don't know, I think great. It helps these beautiful schools to exists. For those of you who are afraid they can not pay their student loans, I, of course, have found the most perfect of all good solutions for this particular problem in this case:

MEXICO WILL PAY OFF YOUR STUDENT LOANS!!!!

I have talked about this with the president of Mexico, very good guy, nice guy, and he has promised to pay for all of it. So much winning!!!!

For the future, I have thought about it, and I have discussed with Ivanka and Melania, very much smarts, truly, very good, and we have decided, we will re-start the Trump University, so that you can, uh, well, you know, study at a good institution for low prizes.

I never understood wind. You know, I know windmills very much. But they're manufactured tremendous — if you're into this — tremendous fumes. Gases are spewing into the atmosphere. You know we have a world, right? So the world is tiny compared to the universe. So tremendous, tremendous amount of fumes and everything. You talk about the carbon footprint — fumes are spewing into the air. Right? Spewing. Whether it's in China, Germany, it's going into the air. It's our air, their air, everything — right? So they make these things, and then they put them up, and if you own a house within vision of some of these monsters, your house is worth 50 percent of the price. They're noisy, they kill the birds. You want to see a bird graveyard? You just go, take a look, a bird graveyard? Go under a windmill some day. You'll see more birds than you've ever seen ever in your life ...

But Oz is a swamp ... There are no intelligent people working here. But if you make me Emperor of Oz, we will Make OZ Great Again: MOGA!!! MOGA!!! MOGA!!!"

When The Trump had completed its ranting, there was, once again, a total silence throughout the crowds as everyone stood there, dumbstruck by the sheer weight of it all.

It was the Rigmaroles who first broke the silence with a resounding cheer. For them, the speech was the pinnacle of what every one of them aspired to do.

The Flutterbudgets, for their part, joined in, though not as enthusiastically as they collectively began focusing on their fears. It was their fears however that The Trump recognized and soon was cajoling them into cheering louder and longer.

Very few of the local citizenry joined in the cheering, preferring to watch and wait.

The Hair had given up all pretense of hiding its existence, instead choosing to stand tall and lash out at anyone that didn't yell loud enough or convincingly enough for its liking.

Chapter 33
Taking Uncle Henry's Advice

Princess Ozma looked back at Her dearest friend in all of Oz, Dorothy Gale of Kansas and smiled softly.

"I would consider that creature to be an Ultracrepidarian," She said confidently.

Over the years, the little farm girl from Kansas had learned many new words while living in Oz, but this one was a new one, even to her. The look on her face told the Princess the same story.

"An Ultracrepidarian is someone who gives opinions on subjects they know nothing about," She informed Her dearest friend.

Dorothy nodded in agreement.

Princess Ozma now addressed the crowd; most of whom were still stunned by the giant peach's bizarre rantings.

"Citizen's of Oz; for the sake of brevity, I will say only that as Emperor, Sir Trump will usher in a new Kakistocracy," Princess Ozma stated confidently.

The effects of Her statement rumbled audibly through the crowd, causing the occasional gasp and laughter.

It was the Flutterbudgets who now led the way in their reactions, though in this instance, theirs was a reaction of fear and consternation. The thought of a government run by the worst, or in this case, the least qualified person in Oz gave them the chills and they fled in masse back southward towards their home and the comfort of solitude it gave them.

Days later, the Flutterbudgets, every man, woman and child, vowed never to leave the confines of Flutterbudget Center ever again.

Meanwhile, The Trump stood there, arms crossed tightly across its chest and pouting profusely as the Flutterbudgets abandoned their position.

"She called me Sir!!! You heard her. I'm your only hope!! Believe me!" The Trump exclaimed. "LIES!!! All lies! It's all FAKE NEWS I tell you! This bitch will kill all of you! Mark my words!!"

Once more, murmurs and gasps rolled through the crowd gathered below. All eyes turned upon Princess Ozma, eager to gauge Her reaction to The Trump's accusations.

"And now, if Uncle Henry's recollections are correct, it's time for a vote," Princess Ozma announced.

With those words, the entirety of Emerald City gathered before the Royal Balcony erupted in cheers and salutations.

Never before had the citizens of Emerald City, nor anyone in the Land of Oz, participated in an actual vote. The excitement was contagious and soon, every corner of Oz, from the Land of the Yips in southern Winkie Country; on across Quadling Country, past the Red Brick Palace of Glinda, Good Witch of the South and Ruler of the Quadling Country; up through Munchkin Country past the Road of Yellow Brick; and on across Gillikin Country and the Great Mountains, everyone was filled with a joy and excitement at the prospect of an election.

Glinda; Good Witch of the South and Ruler of Quadling Country, who had been sitting quietly alongside Dorothy, came forward to assist in the election process.

The hush that had fallen over the entire Emerald City, as well as the Land of Oz was unlike anything anyone in Oz could ever recall before… and Glinda could sense it.

"Citizen's of Oz, speak with one voice as I ask you your vote," Glinda announced. Her voice, as had Princess Ozma's, resounded throughout the Land of Oz.

The Trump came forward, determined to interrupt the proceedings, when Glinda produced her Magic Wand and pointed it at The Hair atop the giant peach.

The Trump backed off and pouted even more so than before.

"If you wish for The Trump to become Emperor of Oz, speak 'yes' now," Glinda declared.

The Rigmaroles began shouting 'YES', over and over as few others joined in. The loudest of them all was

Benson Bailywick, the Keeper of the Gate. Everyone else in attendance watched and waited.

Across the Land of Oz, only a handful shouted 'yes', and even then, only half-heartedly.

Glinda looked about and smiled at Princess Ozma.

"If you wish for Princess Ozma to remain as your Sovereign Ruler, speak 'yes' now," Glinda commanded.

For a scant few seconds, there was total silence across Emerald City and the entire Land of Oz.

Just then, a small mouse, wearing a crown and attended by two mice carrying Her cape appeared upon the parapet of the balcony overlooking the Emerald City.

"YES!!!" proclaimed the Queen of the Field Mice.

What followed next can only be described as pure pandemonium as cries of 'YES" resounded throughout the Land of Oz.

For the next hour, the cries of 'YES" echoed through town halls, mountain valleys, dark forests and the cornfields of Oz.

Chapter 34
The Loser

When silence had been restored to the Emerald City, The Trump immediately launched into a droning tirade.

"Rigged!!! Rigged I tell you!!! This was a fraudulent election! I would've won the popular vote if I was campaigning for the popular vote. I would've gone to where I didn't go at all. I would've gone to where I didn't campaign at all. I would've gone to a couple of places that I didn't go to. And I would've won that much easier than winning the electoral college. But as you know, the electoral college is all that matters. It doesn't make any difference. So, I would've won very, very easily. But it's a different form of winning. You would campaign much differently. You would have a totally different campaign. So, but ..."

The Trump paused for a moment to catch its breath and noticed Princess Ozma looking directly at it.

"There is no electoral college here in Oz and you have lost the election," Princess Ozma stated plainly.

The Trump snorted and stamped about furiously. The Hair also appeared quite agitated with Princess Ozma's pronouncement.

The Rigmaroles joined in, creating quite an uproar as they shouted their displeasure with the outcome of the vote.

"Unfair! Unfair!! Unfair!!!" the Rigmaroles chanted over and over.

"This election was rigged against me! I refuse to accept it! It's all wrong!" The Trump shouted. "Don't you people understand?! I'm the only one who can save you!!!"

The Trump pouted and snarled as the cheering slowly subsided into a dull murmur.

Just then, Professor H. M. Wogglebug, T.E. of the College of Art and Athletic Perfection, showed up with a large parchment.

"If I may interject, the results of the election were quite fair, as the vote count clearly shows," he stated confidently.

"Bullshit!!! All of it is bullshit!!!" The Trump shouted for all to hear. "Fake numbers! Fake results!! Fake creature saying it!!! It's all fake!!!"

A murmur of disappointment ran through the crowd as each began to come to the realization that The Trump was not going to become Emperor of Oz.

The locals manning the wagon soon began to wander off in search of home, be it the Emerald City, Rigmarole Town or somewhere in between.

In time, only a handful of Rigmaroles remained by The Trump's side, chanting its praises and demanding a recount.

The Hair had gone silent, so to speak.

Princess Ozma looked around and noticed that Dorothy was nowhere to be seen.

"I suppose it is time for Aunt Em's advice now..." Princess Ozma thought to Herself. She chuckled softly and noticed Glinda chuckling along with Her.

Chapter 35
Taking Aunt Em's Advice

Billina the Hen turned the corner and looked up to see her dearest friend in the Land of Oz, Dorothy Gale, wearing her Princess Crown and itching to take care of business.

"I know it's a mean creature, but I ain't gonna be bullied by it. You gotta stand up to a bully. Aunt Em said so and she ought'a know," Dorothy explained to Toto, who was rightly worried for her safety. "Besides, I gots me a plan."

Dorothy looked around and saw Billina pecking her way towards her.

"There you are!" she exclaimed. "Are you ready to face down that bully?"

"Are you sure it is who you think it is?" Billina inquired.

"I'm certain of it," Dorothy said confidently. "And you're gonna prove it."

She picked up the little yellow hen and the two of them made for the courtyard where The Trump had taken up residence.

Toto came along for support, though he was more concerned about protecting Dorothy from the creature's advances and its violent tendencies.

By the time the three of them were face-to-face with The Trump, nearly the entire crowd, which had filled the courtyard and then some, were gone. Only a handful of die-hard Rigmaroles remained.

"I'm telling you, they can't deny me being Emperor. It's all in the rules. Read'em. Read the rules. It says so in the rules," The Trump kept insisting to his faithful few, who seem to fawn over its every word.

Princess Ozma and Glinda; Good Witch of the South watched as The Trump paced back and forth, much like a caged animal, but without the cage.

Just then, Dorothy approached The Trump, followed by Toto. Billina, of course, was laying low behind the wagon, awaiting her turn.

"YOU!!!" Dorothy shouted briskly. Her voice was filled with passion and resolve, causing The Trump to back away, despite The Hair trying to goad it into attacking. "You touched Glinda! You broke Countess Von Noritake! You insult everyone around you… and you are a loser!!"

A collective gasp ran through the gathering, including Princess Ozma.

Toto growled very menacingly… and he meant it.

The Trump stood there, dumbstruck by Dorothy's proclamation. The Hair slicked back and watched the little farm girl from Kansas cautiously.

"Time for you to leave Oz… forever!" Dorothy exclaimed. She placed a pair of fingers from her left hand against her lips and gave it all she had.

The whistle that burst forth from Dorothy rang loud and true as it echoed through the walls and roofs and cobblestone streets of Emerald City.

Moments later, Billina the Hen appeared from behind the wagon and clucked loudly.

"Bok! Bok!! Bok!!!" clucked the old yellow hen. "Remember me?"

The Trump stood there, scratching its peach of a head. For once, it had no clue how to deal with what was in front of it.

The Hair however, was instantly reminded of past encounters with the old yellow hen.

"Yes… I see you do remember me. Just as I remember you," clucked Billina. "I also remember that eggs are poison to Nomes… yes?"

With that statement from the old yellow hen, The Hair tugged on the giant peach below, who didn't seem to understand the gravity of the situation. The Hair clearly wanted to be anywhere else but there, yet The Trump didn't seem to get the message.

149

The Hair struggled with the giant peach as Billina watched in silence.

"Allow me," Glinda said politely while retrieving her Magic Wand.

A moment or two later and The Trump and its passenger, The Hair were encased in a giant pink bubble and floating gently above the smooth stone. Both were helpless as everyone else pondered what to do with them.

"Uncle Henry did say to 'vote the bum out', didn't he?" Dorothy asked out loud.

Princess Ozma and Glinda came to the same conclusion at the same time.

"There's no place like home," they spoke in unison.

Glinda flourished her wand beside the bubble and whispered ever so softly.

"There's no place like home…"

The bubble immediately turned south, gaining altitude and speed as it headed southward towards the Mountain of the Hammerheads.

Chapter 36
The Journey Home

The remaining Rigmaroles protested their glorious leader's hasty departure, but none dared challenge Princess Ozma nor Glinda... and especially not Dorothy.

They soon headed for home, weary of the fight and longing for familiar surroundings. The wagon went with them.

The few citizens of Emerald City who remained were most magnanimous in their choice not to ridicule the retreating Rigmaroles. They wished them only the best and made offers to visit and assist any who asked.

It would always be said that the citizens of Emerald City were among the kindest and gentlest of Ozian folk... and they proved it often.

By the time the bubble had made it out of Emerald Country, which surrounds the Emerald City, Princess Ozma and friends had made it back to the Throne Room, where the Magic Picture was showing the bubble's journey across Oz.

"Dorothy, when did you first realize who The Hair on top of that giant peach was?" Princess Ozma inquired politely.

Dorothy thought for a moment before speaking.

"It was an odd thought of a memory from long ago when we met the Nome King and I laughed about his hair."

"Well, I can assure you it wasn't the Nome King that assaulted me earlier," Glinda replied. "That was all on that creature with the head of a giant peach."

Everyone in attendance nodded sadly at her admission.

"Looks like the bubble is about to cross over the Forest of the Fighting Trees," Dorothy observed.

Toto shuddered just a bit as an old memory of his encounter with the Fighting Trees crossed his mind.

It took all of ten minutes for the old forest to be crossed as the pink bubble and its passengers headed slowly up the Mountain of the Hammerheads.

"I should tell you Dorothy that The Hair was not the Nome King himself… just his Beard," Princess Ozma said.

Everyone laughed loud and long at the thought of the Nome King's Beard living on a giant peach.

"But what about the thing beneath the Nome King's Beard?" Dorothy inquired. "Where did that thing come from... and why?"

No one could come up with an answer when the former Wizard of Oz spoke up.

"Well, wherever it came from, I certainly feel sorry for the folks that have to deal with it," the old Wizard said.

Everyone in attendance nodded in agreement.

"Whatever happened to that shovel?" he asked rhetorically.

The Magic Picture, in the mood for a rhetorical answer, now displayed the old wooden shed of a Rigmarole house. In front of it were several citizens of Rigmarole Town, engaged in a long-winded debate about this and that... and even some of the other, as it related to the shovel now held by Benson Bailywick, the Keeper of the Gate.

Soon, the Magic Picture returned to The Trump and its journey out of Oz.

The Court of Princess Ozma watched gleefully as the large pink bubble rose slowly above the Mountain of the Hammerheads and settled down just above the entrance to the cave from whence The Trump had emerged many days before.

"If you would please do the honors, Princess Dorothy," Glinda spoke invitingly as she handed Dorothy a rather long, ornate hat pin.

Dorothy reached forth with the hat pin and poked the large pink bubble that now appeared in the Magic Picture.

Chapter 37
Return From Oz

The Trump felt helpless as it floated across the Land of Oz. It was frustrated at having lost the election, though it could never admit it to itself.

Instead, The Trump focused solely on conspiracy theories, none of which would have made any sense to anyone other than The Trump.

"They're all against me..." the creature with the head of a giant peach kept thinking to itself.

It watched as the Ozian countryside passed beneath its feet and noticed that the Mountain of the Hammerheads seemed to be getting closer and closer.

"Not the knuckleheads again?" The Trump shouted within the confines of the large pink bubble.

It watched as the bubble passed over a large, dark forest and slowly rose up to greet the Mountain of the Hammerheads.

The Hammerheads scurried about as the bubble passed slowly over their heads. They lobbed all manner of insults and threats at it as it made for the large cave entrance, which the Hammerheads feared.

When the large pink bubble came to a slow, graceful stop and hovered gently above the cave entrance, The Trump felt an odd, familiar feeling, as though it was just on the edge of falling asleep.

Just then, the large pink bubble popped and The Trump suddenly found itself falling into the dark of the cave.

The Trump watched as the light from the entrance of the cave faded away while it fell into the long dark tunnel that had brought it here.

In no time at all, The Trump was in total darkness and the odd, familiar feeling of falling asleep took over as the giant peach faded into slumber.

The Nome King's Beard had decided that now was the time to part company with the creature it had encountered travelling through its underground realm days before.

Moments later, The Beard had detached itself from the giant peach and floated away into a nearby crack in the tunnel, which had been its home for over a century. There it returned to a life of solitude, content to know that the up-stairs people were still quite insane.

The Trump snored its way down the long dark tunnel, dreams of cackling laughter and chants of MAGA filling its head when it came to a sudden stop.

Donald J. Trump, President of the United States of America, awoke with a start in the Lincoln Bedroom, where he had decided to spend the night before.

All he could see was white. He looked around, still foggy from sleep and saw only white.

He reached up and dragged the chicken bucket off of his head and saw the television blaring in front of him.

"Whew!" he sighed. "Thought I went blind there for a moment."

Around him were the remains of numerous hamburger wrappers and diet soda cans. A pile of used-up Sharpie's sat in the far corner next to the pile of used-up lip balm tubes. The lip balm tubes, of course, were discarded by the various staff members, cabinet members, senators and congressional members, who would use them prior to kissing Donald's ass.

"Ugh!" Donald groaned to himself. "Was it all just a dream?"

He glared at the television screen and was delighted to see his favorite show, Fox News, was alive and doing well.

Sean Hannity was interviewing some trivial guest who was talking about Roger Stone and Michael Cohen, thus prompting the obligatory stock photo of each.

Donald stared hard at the screen, stunned by the images of Hannity, Cohen and Stone.

"How could it be a dream?" he whispered to himself as he pointed at the screen. *"You were there... and you... and you were there too."*

The End